THE FAE LORD

The Fae Court

Book 2

ALEXIS BROOKE

Editing by Quinn Nichols, Quill & Bone Editing

Book Cover by Krafigs Design

ISBN:

Paperback - 978-1-916671-32-4

Hardback - 978-1-916671-33-1

For those of us that prefer fifty shades of fae…

ONE

Alana

His lips trail a hot, torturous line down my throat. He tugs at my dress, my nipples pebbling with the anticipations of his touch. But instead of caressing them, he lets his hands levitate over my body. I lean into him – desperate to feel him. But he does not give in.

Instead, he tightens the bonds around my wrists and shakes his head. "You will not come until I tell you to, Alana, do you understand?"

I fix my eyes on his, but do not reply. I want his wrath. I want him to punish me with his pleasure.

His gaze darkens, his eyes narrow. He smiles then and tweaks his thumb under my chin. My dress is open, my breasts exposed to the cool night-time air. He looks down and licks his lips. Then he thrusts his hand between my thighs and cups my pussy, hard. He does not move it, just applies pressure that sends waves of heat to my core, and continues to stare into my eyes.

"Tell me you understand?"

Finally, I nod. "I understand, my lord."

I expect him to touch me, a reward for giving him the answer he wanted. Instead, he beats his wings and kneels down in front of me. He lifts my skirts and blows warm air onto my clit. I sigh and my eyes roll back as I sink into the anticipation of his tongue.

He does not give it to me.

He takes his index finger and runs it gently through my folds, gathering my wetness, then he looks up at me, reaches up, and makes me suck his finger into my mouth.

"How do you taste?" he asks.

"Why don't you find out for yourself?" I swirl my tongue around the tip of my finger, teasing him, knowing this answer will drive him wild. Then I watch as he tilts his head, considers his next move, and finally gives me what I need . . . his tongue.

With expertly torturous slowness, he kisses the inside of my thighs. When he finally licks my clit, making perfect circles before tugging it gently with his teeth, a vicious moan escapes my lips and my body arches towards him.

Except, I can't move because he has me tied too tightly. All I can do is writhe beneath his mouth as he explores all the ways he can make me feel.

When he stands and starts to take off his clothes, I am shaking. My breasts long for his touch, and I long to touch him.

He peels off his shirt, exposing his perfectly chiselled torso.

I want to lick his stomach all the way down until I reach his cock.

He unfastens his belt and drops his pants to the floor. He is not wearing any underwear.

I take in the sight of him because I have never seen him like this before; fully exposed in front of me. He is glorious. His silver hair hangs loose over his shoulders. Every inch of him makes me feel like he could both destroy me and claim me and worship me.

My eyes drop to his cock, admiring his length. Then my breath catches in my chest. He is pierced, and suddenly there is nothing I want more than to swirl my tongue over his metal and to feel it inside me.

How did I not notice before? In the tunnels? Was I so overcome with pleasure that I couldn't even tell what was happening inside my own body? Was every sensation so overwhelming that it was impossible to know where they were coming from and what was causing them?

I strain against the ties that bind me to the wooden post.

Eldrion beats his wings and rises up into the air, drawing closer until his cock is level with my mouth. He treads the air just in front of my face, just out of reach. I stick out my tongue, desperate to reach him, but he simply smirks and refuses to move closer.

"Please . . ." I open my mouth again. This time, while he fists his dick, he lets me take his balls into my mouth. I groan as I suck and tease them.

He groans too.

Then he grabs my hair and jerks my head back. He stares at me for a moment, then strokes my cheek. Tender. Loving.

A look that makes me hate him even more. Because how can he look at me like that when he has evil in his veins?

The look lasts only a second before he bends down and kisses me. Hard. Searching. He grabs hold of my face, then finally he lowers himself to the floor and begins to kiss my breasts, my nipples.

I want to touch myself. I need to touch myself.

I can feel the wetness pooling between my thighs.

Eldrion raises his head and meets my gaze. Then he lifts my leg and, without warning, thrusts up inside me.

He holds my hands still, never breaking eye contact with me.

He thrusts again, then slips his free hand between us to play with my clit.

I call his name – shout it like a curse word – and it disappears in the air between us, swallowed by the moans that reverberate in my chest as pleasure sweeps like molten silver through my body, destroying my resolve.

My muscles tense.

The pleasure is too much.

"Please, I need to come, let me come . . ."

Eldrion looks as if he is considering taking his hand away. Instead, he unties the bonds, turns me around, and grabs hold of my hips. He jerks me back onto his cock and reaches around to torture my clit with his fingers while his wings caress my breasts. Mine are pressed flat between us, and the pressure sends ripples of static pleasure skittering down my spine.

I can't think.

I can't breathe.

All I know is that I'm about to be pushed over the edge, and he's going to push me there, and that nothing in the world feels like this.

Because I have never wanted anyone the way I want him.

Or hated anyone the way I hate him.

Eldrion slams into me hard, his cock touching the place inside me that makes everything go fuzzy and dark and my brain feel like it's dissociating from my body.

When I come, I scream his name again but this time it sounds different. I tip my head back and he curls his fingers around my throat. He kisses my forehead. He kisses my neck, just below my ear, and he holds me close as I tremble against him.

Then he mutters, "Alana . . ." He pushes me forward, holding me up with his wings, and shakes as his orgasm takes hold of him. With his arms curled around me, he breathes hard against my neck. I am completely engulfed my him. He is inside me, and around me. Everything is him. There is nothing else.

But then he starts to fade.

Something shifts.

I look down. His arms have become translucent, dark, grey. His wings become smoke. It flutters away into the air.

I turn around, spinning to face him.

He opens his mouth and a cloud of shadows spills from inside it.

I reach for him.

I scream for him.

And then he is gone.

I am alone. I look down. There are no bonds around my wrists. My clothes are back on my body. I am surrounded by trees and someone else is calling my name. Not Eldrion.

"Alana?" Briony's voice. It floats towards me through the trees.

"Alana . . ." I mutter, hearing my name as if Eldrion is speaking it. I pinch the bridge of my nose. "What is happening to me?"

My legs are still quivering as I weave my way through the trees towards Briony's voice. I find her by the campfire. She looks worried but relaxes when she sees me. "You know we're supposed to travel in pairs," she says, reaching for my hand,

I take hers only briefly, still quivering with the memory of Eldrion's touch.

Except, it wasn't his touch.

Was it?

I rub my temples.

How am I supposed to know what is real? Since he gave me that vision, or I saw it, or whatever the hell happened in those tunnels, I've been having them more and more frequently.

Dreams about him.

Nightmares about the world ending.

I don't know if he's making me see them or if something else is happening.

I took Kayan's powers. Is it possible I took Eldrion's, too? Is he seeing what I'm seeing?

Something inside me feels dull and empty every time I realise I have been dreaming and that he's not really here with me. It feels as if he is too far away, as if there is an invisible thread pulling me towards him, vicious voices in my head telling me to go to him.

One in particular. It could be his. It could be mine. It sounds like both and neither.

It whispers to me on the wind.

Go to him. Find him. You have to find him, Alana.

Briony tugs my sleeve. "Alana? You look like you've seen a ghost." I shake my head. She looks more ghostly than I do. She is pale and drawn. We have survived on little food for the past three weeks.

Trapped within our small protection shield, hiding from Eldrion's gaze in the deepest part of the woods outside of Luminael, there are too many of us and not enough wildlife or edible vegetation to sustain us.

Yes, we have the river, thank goodness. But water will not sustain us forever.

"How are the Leafborne?" I ask.

The camp is very much divided. The Shadowkind are suspicious of us. We are suspicious of them.

I say *we* . . .

I am not one of them. Despite everything, my kin still do not trust me. I am neither Shadowkind nor Leafborne. I float between them, and both groups look at me with disgust.

Finn, as always, is the only one who treats me with kindness. Although, I wish he would treat me with more than kindness if I'm honest. He has barely touched me since we arrived here, and I'm not sure if it's because we're in such close quarters with the others or because something has changed.

I wonder if I was more . . . satisfied . . . whether the dreams of Eldrion would be fewer. Whether Finn could fuck Eldrion out of my head.

But I haven't told him about them. I can't.

If he knew what I saw and what Eldrion and I did in the tunnels . . . I swallow hard. It feels like a betrayal. Finn would see it as a betrayal. It *is* a betrayal.

My body betrayed me, and I betrayed Finn.

Perhaps the others are right; perhaps I am a monster.

Briony starts to walk towards the food station, where we take it in turns to volunteer as chefs and to hand out rations. She takes a cup of nettle tea and wrinkles her nose at the lack of sugar. She drinks it down anyway, but I opt for my one portion of walnut coffee.

No milk. No sugar, but better than nettles.

We find a space next to the fire and sit beside one another.

We are the only mixed friendship out of the two groups of fae. No one else has dared to cross the divide, and I appreciate Briony more than I can make her understand. The fact she has not shied away from me shows she is a true friend.

"Spirits are low," she mutters. "The Leafborne accused the Shadowkind of giving themselves greater rations at breakfast." She pauses and looks at me furtively from the corner of her eye. "You have been gone since breakfast. Where have you been?"

"Just walking," I answer quickly. "Nowhere. And everywhere." I smile slowly and sip my coffee. "Within the bounds of the shield, of course."

Briony grimaces and sips her tea, then grimaces harder.

"Has Finn spoken to you about our next steps? I tried to talk to him about it, but he is reluctant. He says he is still thinking, and waiting on news from the elves."

"The elves . . ." Briony rolls her eyes. "They have never been trustworthy. I still don't understand why–" her words are broken off when Finn appears opposite us. Striding in front of the fire, he looks angry, his steps wide, his stance stiff and forceful.

He doesn't even look in my direction, just marches over to a small group of Leafborne and grabs one of them by the throat. Hauling them to their feet, he stares down into their face and spits, "You accuse us of being unfair?"

The Leafborne, Pen, tries to pull away, but Finn is athletic and strong, despite his small wings. The piercings on their tips jingle as he draws himself taller and wider.

"No, I . . ." Pen replies shakily.

Finn's jaw twitches. "If you accuse the Shadowkind, you accuse me. I am their leader."

I sense Briony twitch a little beside me. Was she aware that's how Finn had declared himself?

"I apologise," Pen says tightly. "I only thought –"

Finn lets him go. His eyes soften, and I see an almost visible wave of regret wash over him. He shakes his head, then puts a firm hand on Pen's shoulder. "I'm sorry," he says. "I apologise, Pen. Tensions are high. I am as hungry and tired as the rest of you, and as frustrated by being stuck here for so long with no progress. I overreacted. Please accept my apologies."

Pen nods but narrows his eyes at Finn as if he doesn't quite believe him.

I stand and walk quickly over, thrusting my cup into Briony's hands so mine are free.

"Not now, Alana," Pen snaps. "I don't need you manipulating me into not being angry with your boyfriend." He glances at my fingers as if I'm going to attempt to cast a spell on him right this second.

"That's not what I was trying to do. I was simply –"

Pen shakes his head, looks at me with disgust, and turns to walk away. The other Leafborne are muttering. Maura is the only one who continues to stare at me. I desperately want to let my gates down and search her feelings; to see if she really still hates me, despite everything. But if I do that, she'll know. She'll sense it, and I will have proved them all right.

They believe their thoughts aren't safe around me.

I can't do anything to fuel their fear.

As I inhale sharply, pain lodging between my ribs, Finn puts his hand on the base of my spine. "Ignore him. Ignore all of them. They'll see what you are eventually." He kisses the side of my cheek. "They'll worship you eventually. You'll see."

I lean into him and sigh. He smells so good, and he feels so warm and familiar.

He is the only one who has truly seen me for who I am. He gives me exactly what I need, whenever I need it.

I owe him the truth about Eldrion, and the tunnels, and the visions.

But what if telling him means losing him forever?

TWO

Eldrion

The elf is sweating. Beads of perspiration drip down his pale face, and he grimaces as I lean in closer.

"Fuck you, Eldrion," he spits.

My eyes flash. Anger settles deeper between my ribs. He knows where they are. The elves know everything. And he will tell me before the day is out. Or he will lose his life.

I stalk away, slowly, rolling up my sleeves.

It's dark, and it stinks in this hellhole of a place.

It's unusual to find an elf in this part of the city, which is why I know he has the connections I need. Connections to the whispers that have been rippling through Luminael ever since she escaped from my clutches.

Ever since my power was questioned.

For the first time in centuries, there are rumours of an

uprising. I showed weakness. I allowed them to escape. And now I am paying the price.

I rub my temples. My visions have both abandoned me and intensified. They show me nothing new. Only what I already know. And what they do show me grows ever more terrifying.

I don't know if this means the city's fate is growing closer to being sealed, or if it means I am simply running out of time to reverse it. Perhaps it means it is already set in motion. It always has been. Perhaps every step I take simply draws me – and my people – closer to oblivion.

I have thought of my mother very little since she died. She was not a kind woman or the sort of mother who cherished her children. She made it clear I was an inconvenience. A speck she would rather not have to deal with. She saw nothing good or powerful in me. To her, I was weak.

But now, for the first time, I find myself wishing she was here so I could ask her what to do. Because she was, if nothing else, wise. She understood how to interpret her visions in a way I never have. Perhaps because I never had anyone to teach me.

Mine didn't start until after she died. Perhaps that is why she hated me; because I was inadequate. Perhaps I wish she had been alive to see what I grew into.

Perhaps I don't.

I rub my temples again. My thoughts feel as though they are not my own. They swirl and spiral and twist inside my skull like dark, suffocating smoke. I cannot see through them and I cannot determine what's real.

All I know – with resounding certainty – is that I need Alana back.

She is important. *She* is the missing piece.

And she saw what I saw.

I spin around and flex my fingers. Ink-like smoke twirls around them. I use my powers infrequently. I prefer to rule through the anticipation of violence rather than the use of it. And though I've used brute strength on plenty of occasions, my shadow magic is something usually reserved for battle.

But the elf has left me no choice.

His eyes widen as I draw closer to him. Sitting on a wooden stool in the centre of the abandoned inn I sequestered last night, he cannot move. I bound his wrists and ankles with copper. He is lucky I have not yet taken his ability to speak.

"Are you prepared for what you're about to endure?" I ask, peering into his eyes, feeling my own flash like shards of silver ice, boring into his soul.

The elf's jaw twitches. He thinks he can withstand it. He thinks he can be brave.

He is wrong.

I have not used this element of my powers for two centuries. Am I sorry I'm using it now? No. For her, I would infect every soul in this city until their insides cracked and withered and they were unable to keep their secrets from me.

I turn my palms up and, again, flex my fingers. The smoke drifts towards him. It starts at his ankles and weaves its way up his body, coiling around his limbs. He winces as the smoke squeezes his calves. He inhales sharply and shifts on the stool.

I tilt my head but remain completely still. When I breathe out, the smoke begins to move faster. It swirls thicker and darker. It reaches his throat, and the vein on the side of his neck throbs. It reaches his lips, and he tries to keep them shut. It pries them open and drags a quivering scream from somewhere deep in his soul.

His head tips back, his mouth opens, the shadows enter him.

They claim him.

They sweep through his veins, and nestle inside him, and scrape like acid until he screams again.

"Tell me, elf, where are the Leafborne hiding?"

The elf shakes his head. He has no loyalty to them; elves know everything and are loyal to no one, so why is he lying to me? Why would he risk his life for them?

"Where are the Shadowkind?"

Again, he shakes his head. He grips the sides of the chair tighter as his eyes roll back and darken. "Fuck," he cries, "you . . . *my lord.*"

I do not let my anger take over.

I walk forward, then place a hand firmly on his arm. My wings splay out to my sides, casting dark shadows over his smooth, pale face. Then I touch his temple, and let the pain intensify.

The shadows clamour inside him, swell, push, crack, break.

He screams.

Then the screams stop. He is panting, unable to make a sound because all he can see is the pain.

I exhale slowly and breathe a cloud of warm, soothing air over his skin.

He cranes his head around and stares into my eyes.

I give him barely a second before I start the process all over again. Smoke, ink, congealing inside him, breaking him from the inside out. Then sunlight. Compassion.

The cycle continues until close to dawn.

Finally, he blinks at me. His entire body is trembling. His mouth hangs open. "Thank you," he whispers. "Thank you for making it stop."

"Tell me where the Shadowkind and the Leafborne are hiding, and I'll never have to hurt you again."

He stares at me for a moment, then he starts to cry. "I would tell you, my lord. But I don't know. I promise you, I don't know."

He is telling the truth. An overwhelming sense of certainty washes over me. As if his true thoughts and feelings are floating in the air between us.

The elf does not lie.

My wings beat hard behind me. The air cools his face. I untie his bonds. He sighs with relief and droops forward, rubbing his wrists.

"Thank you," he mutters. "Thank you for showing mercy."

My gut twists. Mercy?

No.

I study him for a moment.

Then I slit his throat, and leave him there, his silvery blood dripping in thick, heavy droplets onto the floor at his feet.

THREE

Alana

Sunlight blinds me. I am standing above the city, looking down, but I can't see. I blink into the sun. It pummels my eyelids, forcing them closed.

I grip the edge of the roof. The spot where Kayan stood before he died.

Eldrion is beside me. I know it is him because I feel his presence, like a dark, ominous shadow, ready to engulf me.

It is unbearably hot. Beads of perspiration cling to my brow, and my dress hugs my hips tightly. I scream. A loud, bone-rattling scream. Something is making fear course through my body. I cannot latch onto it. It is a feeling, a presence, a *thing* that threatens to destroy every fibre in my body.

A hand takes mine. Why is Eldrion touching me like that? Why is he trying to comfort me? I turn, snatching my wrist from his grasp, and pull a knife from my skirt. I hold it to his throat.

Now, I can see.

The light is fading, becoming darker.

His eyes glisten, silver against grey.

He is smoke, and fury, and the way he looks at me, it's as if he wants to kill me and fuck me and can't decide which to choose.

He does not flinch or try to fight me. He just looks down at my blade and says, "End me if you dare."

The muscles in my forearm twitch. I inhale deeply. I thrust forward.

And then I am somewhere else.

Standing on charred earth, legs shaking. The noise is unbearable. The noise in my head. Screaming, and screaming, and screaming. And they are not just my screams. They are screams that belong to everyone. Every single creature in the city is screaming.

Bodies lie at my feet. Blood pools in deep crevices on the ground.

The sky is black. Dark clouds gather. Thunder shakes the air. Rain begins to fall, and it bleeds into the crimson puddles, spreading the darkness further and further, and coating the ground like poisonous tar.

More darkness approaches. A huge, looming shadow.

At first I think it's him – Eldrion – but then I realise it is something more. It is water. A tidal wave, approaching the city. Coming to engulf us all.

I try to fly but my wings beat with futile effort behind me.

I try to hold the water back using Kayan's magic. The magic that saved us in the tunnels. But it is no use.

I can still hear the screams. They torment me, they threaten to break me.

They will not stop.

"Alana . . ."

My name. The sound is familiar, but I can barely latch onto it amongst the clamour of noise beating against the raw insides of my skull.

"Alana . . ."

"Alana . . ."

My eyes spring open. My heart is beating so hard inside my ribs that I feel as if it might break free and drop down at my feet. I am freezing cold, but drenched in sweat. My hands are shaking.

Beside me, Finn smooths my hair from my face and kisses the bridge of my nose. He takes my hands in his and meets my eyes, trying to pull me back into the present. "Alana, you were having a nightmare." He is whispering, talking to me like a child he is trying to comfort. He takes a flask of whisky from beside the bed and hands it to me. I drink down a large swig and wince as it burns my throat. "The same one?" he asks, taking the flask and drinking some himself.

I can hardly speak, but manage to nod, while still clinging on to his hand.

"What do they mean?" I ask him. Because surely he knows. He has to; he's the one with all the plans, all the ideas.

He shakes his head and pulls the blanket tightly around us, curling in behind me and hugging my waist as I settle back into his embrace.

"When you and Eldrion fought in the tunnels," he whispers, "what happened?"

"Why does that matter?" I ask, swallowing hard as guilt, like bile, congeals in my throat.

"Because there are rumours that Eldrion's powers involve the power of prophecy." Finn is speaking quietly, close to my ear, his breath warm and sweet. "If you fought, perhaps, somehow . . ." He stops, shaking his head. "No, it's silly."

"What is?" I frown at him.

"Absorbing Kayan's power was one thing. Absorbing Eldrion's? He's too powerful. There's no way . . ."

I sit up, tucking my knees up underneath me. "You think I absorbed his power?" A trickle of something that borders on the precipice between intrigue and fear drips down my spine.

Finn shakes his head. "I don't see how," he says. "It would make sense, but you absorbed Kayan's powers when you fucked him, right?" He meets my eyes.

A sickening sense of guilt swills inside me.

"Right," I whisper.

"So, unless . . ." Finn raises his eyebrows, but then his lips quirk into a smile. "Alana, you can tell me. If something happened between you . . ." His smile drops a little. "As long as he didn't hurt you." A darkness tinges his voice.

"He didn't hurt me." I reach for Finn's hands and clasp them tightly. "But we . . ." I can't force the words out. I can't. I look down, shaking my head. "I don't know how or why. I hate him. I hate him so much, Finn, but –"

When I look up, Finn is studying me with an expression I haven't seen before. He inches closer, curling his arms around my waist. "You fucked him in the tunnels?"

I nod, but as I watch Finn's face, I do not feel guilty. I feel . . . intrigued.

He slides his hand between my legs and lets it settle there. He doesn't move his fingers, just cups my pussy with his palm and applies a little pressure. "Did it feel good?"

My breath hitches in my chest. I nod, unable to speak.

"Did he make you come?"

My lips part and a small, breathy murmur escapes. I stroke Finn's face, then lean in to kiss him. As my mouth meets his, I whisper, "Yes, he made me come."

Finn grabs me and pulls me into his lap.

He grips my waist tightly, crushing me against his chest. He feels different to Eldrion; athletic instead of muscular, but still strong. His mouth devours mine, his tongue exploring my mouth, tasting me with an urgency that makes my entire body shiver. I wrap my arms around his neck, feeling him grow hard beneath me.

His hand between my leg shifts, his fingers now gently stroking my folds. Arousal starts to vibrate in my core. I tilt my pelvis, seeking his touch. Wanting more. I moan into his mouth, heat spreading between my legs as the memory of Eldrion's fierce embrace in the tunnels merges with the way Finn is touching me.

"Did you enjoy it?" Finn growls against my lips. His voice is raspy and deep; it carries a tone I haven't heard before. "Did you enjoy having Lord Eldrion's cock inside you? Did you enjoy knowing you have the power to make him yours?"

I nod, unable to speak. My breath is coming in quick bursts. Did I make Eldrion mine? Is that what happened? Did he want me so much that he forgot he hates me?

"You enjoyed it, didn't you?" Finn's voice hardens, but there is a sparkle in his eyes that tells me he is teasing me. His gaze locks with mine. Curiosity quivers on his skin. His wings, small and tattered, quiver too. And the bells chime.

I nod again, unable to hold back the truth any longer.

As guilt swirls inside me, Finn's fingers continue to explore my sensitive flesh. His other hand moves to my hair, gripping the back of my head and pulling me closer, pressing his forehead against mine as he starts to fuck me with his fingers.

"I'm going to make you come, Alana," he growls.

Fuck, I love it when he's like this. I need him like this. I need him to stop the voices swirling in my head, and the visions, and the thoughts. I need him to fuck me until I don't know where I am or who I am.

"I'm going to make you come so hard you forget about him. I'm going to show you what it means to be with someone who loves you."

I grind down onto his hand, moaning again, pulling him closer because he is still not close enough.

As his fingers delve deeper, my eyes flutter shut. I can feel his knuckles pressing against my inner walls. Stroking. Probing. His thumb caresses my clit, sending waves of pleasure coursing through me.

"Tell me, Alana," he whispers. "Tell me what you liked about his touch."

My heart races. Surely, he does not want to hear this? But as I meet his gaze, and he grins at me, I realise he does. He really does want to hear this.

"It was . . . different. Intense. Like he wasn't sure whether he hated me or needed me."

Finn's eyes darken. He tugs my hair. "And you liked the way he fucked you?"

I nod again, breathless.

"Tell me how he did it."

"Standing, up against the wall of the tunnel. He fucked me so hard the tunnels collapsed."

Finn's eyes widen. In one swift movement, he pulls me off his lap and tosses me down on the blankets beneath us. He strips off his clothes, revealing his toned body and his hard cock.

I devour him hungrily. I want him inside me. I need him inside me.

"Tell me what you want, Alana." He kneels, towering over me. "Tell me how you want me to fuck you."

I wriggle into the blankets and part my legs for him. "I want you to fuck me so hard I can barely breathe. Like he did. Fuck me like you own me."

Finn's grin widens. A look of pure hunger glistens in his eyes. He crawls on top of me. His body presses against mine. His lips devour me. He bites my throat, my nipples, my lower lip. He explores every inch of my skin.

"Are you ready to forget about him now, Alana?" he asks, staring down at me.

I search for him with my hips, desperate for him to fill me up.

He positions himself at my entrance, his cock throbbing as it presses against me. I feel his warmth. The anticipation building as I open my legs wider for him.

Eyes darkening, Finn hooks one of my legs over his shoulder, then the other, and then he plunges into me. He holds me steady and thrusts harder. I slip my hand between us and make furious circles around my clit.

Our bodies slap together, our moans fill the air

My orgasm starts to build.

I cry out, not caring if anyone hears us.

Finn releases my legs, grabs my arms and slams them down above my head, holding them tightly as he pummels into me.

Pleasure builds like a tornado inside me. A primitive scream escapes my lips as pleasure becomes pain and then pleasure again.

Finn meets my eyes, then holds my chin steady. "Come for me, Alana. Come on my cock."

I jerk onto him, then wrap my arms around his neck and cling on tightly as I descend into exquisite oblivion.

He does not come inside me. Instead, he gives me his cock and makes me drink down every last drop of his cum. I drink hungrily, taking him deep to the back of my throat.

When I swallow, panting, he kisses my forehead.

"Fuck," he says, flopping down beside me. "I never knew the idea of you with someone else would make me so . . ."

I giggle, tucking myself into his arms. For the first time in weeks, I feel free. There is no sneaking guilt burrowing into my chest. "Feral?" I ask, my pussy still throbbing with the memory of how he pounded it.

He nods, sighing, rubbing his chest with his palm.

I look up, meeting his eyes. "You really aren't cross?"

He shakes his head. "Shadowkind are a little more free than you Leafborne," he chuckles. "We don't necessarily believe in one mate for everyone."

I frown at him. This surprises me.

"Eldrion? I mean, I could have picked someone a little less . . . evil . . . for you to fuck. But it still works." He looks down at his cock. It's growing hard again. He quirks his eyebrows at me. "Want me to show you again how much I don't mind?"

He settles between my legs, this time running his tongue over the remains of my wetness.

I sigh and sink back into the pillows. “Yes. Please. Show me.”

FOUR

Eldrion

I can still smell the elf's blood on my hands as I stride back to the castle. I choose to walk. I want to taste the air and hear the whispers.

It is late. Dark. Everything is closed up tight. There is no curfew in place, but the Sunborne, and the Shadowkind who live in servitude to them, have taken it upon themselves to go into hiding at night. As if they can feel something coming.

Sunborne are powerful. We are the most powerful.

But as far as I know, there has never been another who can see the future. Only my family. Only my mother, and me.

And only one who can command the shadows. Not even my brother could do that.

I stop in front of a tavern. Its doors and windows are shuttered closed, but there is movement pulsating within. The scent of liquor drifts out from beneath the door and the cracks in the window frame.

I haven't been inside a tavern since I ascended to the throne at one hundred years old. I have barely set foot outside of the castle, and in recent months, my hermit-like lifestyle has been even more intense.

I turn the handle and push. The door is locked.

I look up at the place where, on the other side, the bolt will be sealing it shut and hear it slide to one side.

I keep my powers a mystery as far as I can. I rule through the threat of what they might do, the anticipation of them. I show them how cruel I am with my bare hands and let them imagine what this would mean if I was using magic.

No one knew about my mother's visions. No one knows about mine.

That is the way I like it.

I push my shoulder into the door and as soon as I enter, allow my wings to unfurl.

They fill the space in front of me.

Over by the fireplace, the patrons look up with wide eyes.

This is a Shadowkind tavern, but it is Sunborne who are in front of me. They stand immediately, assessing my silver hair and my black wings. They know who I am.

Behind the bar, the innkeeper says, "My lord. It is a pleasure to have you in –"

I shake my head and raise my palm to stop him talking. I do not care to hear what he has to say. "Whisky," I say, sitting down on a stool at the bar.

The Sunborne who were playing what looks like a game of

runes are muttering in hushed voices as if they are unsure whether to talk to me or carry on with their game.

I snap my fingers at them and tell them to continue as they were. "I do not wish to be disturbed," I say, stalking into the corner of the tavern and choosing a table that faces out towards the rest of the room.

Folding myself into the large leather armchair behind the table, I let my fingers rest on the scratched and peeling material. I pick at it as I drink my whisky. And I strain my ears.

They do not know I can hear them. They have no idea that I can hear their voices as if they are whispering right next to my ear, that I can control shadows, and see the future.

They do not know half of what I'm capable of.

Perhaps I don't either.

I drink slowly.

At first, they talk only about the game, but as the hours wear on and their bellies become more full of alcohol, their tongues loosen.

"The elves are muttering something about an uprising," one of them says, glancing in my direction. I do not give any indication that I have heard them, simply keep my gaze cast down into my glass.

"An uprising? You mean the Shadowkind?" another says. He has thick glasses, a pinched, pale face, and large teeth. His wings twitch as he speaks. "I told Marta to keep a close eye on ours."

The one who mentioned the uprising shifts her playing piece, takes a sip of ale, and shrugs. "That is what I've heard," she says. "At the market this morning, at least half the stalls were empty. They are disappearing. You must have noticed?"

"There are rumours that Eldrion lost *all* of his," says a man with thick curly hair. "All of them gone from the castle. That's why the banquets have stopped. He's got no servants left to serve and no jester left to entertain."

The woman lifts her ale to her lips and takes a large drink. When she puts it back down on the table, she shrugs. "I also heard that the Leafborne escaped. The slaves from the auction."

"He must be losing his touch," chuckles the one in glasses.

"Careful, Brock, he's only over there."

Brock simply chuckles again. "And I am supposed to be afraid? He's losing it. He lost control of this city a long time ago."

My heart is beating hard against my ribs, and it is taking every ounce of willpower I possess not to rise from this table and rip off their wings.

When they leave, staggering out into the cloying heat of the night – because in Luminael, the warmth of the day seems to swell and amplify after dark – I stride over to the bar and slam down my tankard.

The innkeeper pours me another without saying a word.

As I take it from him, he glances at my hands and spots the silvery blood on my fingertips. Just the tiniest drop, nestled into the crevice beside my fingernail. He swallows hard then, as if on purpose, and adjusts the cap he's wearing.

I notice his ears.

Of course, he's an elf. Most who run taverns and businesses in Luminael are; the Sunborne are too lofty for such pursuits and the Shadowkind haven't been allowed to run businesses for centuries.

"What did they do?" The innkeeper leans forward onto the bar, steepling his fingers, and meets my eyes.

If he was afraid of me when I entered, perhaps the Sunbornes' conversation changed things. Or perhaps he is now more angry than afraid.

"He did not give me the answer I was looking for." I take a swig of ale, then purse my lips.

"What was the question?" the innkeeper asks.

I study him for a moment. There is something strange about this elf. I cannot tell whether he is trying to help me, extort me, or if he's simply curious.

For the second time in the space of twenty-four hours, a strange sensation washes over me. Thoughts that aren't my own drift into my mind. Not thoughts . . . feelings.

Curiosity, titillation . . . smugness.

This elf knows something. But I don't need to torture him for answers. He *wants* to give me what I need.

"I am looking for the Shadowkind and the Leafborne who escaped from the castle." I draw back my shoulders and study him carefully.

The elf seems surprised that I have spoken so openly about something that, until now, has been only whispered of in the alleys and dark passageways of the city.

"Everyone knows they escaped. There is no sense in me pretending otherwise."

"And you want them back." The elf pours himself a glass of whisky, then one for me too.

I shove aside the ale and accept the spirit instead.

"So you can make an example of them . . . like the one you threw from the barricades?" The elf folds his arms, standing up straight. "I saw it. Brutal." He shakes his head, but not a single ounce of fear or sorrow emanates from him.

"No. Not for that." I sniff the whisky, then down it in one. "There is one particular fae I need. I do not care what happens to the rest."

"I could help you with that." The elf extends his hand now, offering to shake mine. "My name's Garratt. I've run this place for years. I have . . ." He pauses, quirking an eyebrow at me. "Connections."

"Are you trustworthy, Garratt?" I am three times larger than this elf, and a hundred times more powerful. Yet, in this moment, brute strength means nothing. I know, without a shadow of a doubt, that Garratt would not care if I tortured him. He has the air of someone who is on this earth to extract what they can from it and has accepted that death will come sooner or later.

Which means the only thing I have to bargain with is power or money.

"No," he says frankly, grimacing into his whisky glass. "Not in the least. But for a long time now, I've been wanting to . . ." He wrinkles his nose. "How shall I phrase it? *Enhance* my status around here."

Here we go . . . Power. He wants power.

I wait for him to continue.

"Make me head of the elven police, and I'll find your fae for you."

"Elven police?" I scoff loudly. "There is no such thing. Elves are not known for their law enforcement skills." I pause and tap my fingers on the side of my glass. "You aren't asking to form a guard, you're asking for permission to run the underbelly of the city."

Garratt tilts his head from side to side. "See," he says, gesturing to the table where the Sunborne were sitting, "I knew you hadn't lost your touch." He taps his temple. "Still got it."

For a moment, anger begins to sizzle beneath my skin. But then, as I study this cocky elf, a laugh blooms instead. "I like you, Garratt." I tip my glass at him, then gesture for him to fill it. "You have balls of steel, I'll give you that."

Shrugging, Garratt says, "Nothing to lose. You either agree, and my little empire grows overnight, or you kill me and, well, I won't know any better then, will I?" He hands me my glass back.

"Very wise." I hesitate, then nod at him. "Very well. Elven police. Why not? But hear me, you will have no jurisdiction over the Sunborne. You are to police the Shadowkind only. Watch them, make sure they are not gathering in groups, talking in the shadows, plotting . . ." I pause, inhaling sharply.

"Plotting to overthrow their rulers," the elf finishes my sentence for me. "I understand." He extends his hand to shake mine.

"Your first priority will be to find the ones who escaped from the castle."

Garratt nods again. "Top of the list, my lord."

"And in return?" I squeeze his hand tightly, but he does not flinch. "What do you want from me, elf?"

"Oh, that's easy." Garratt squeezes back. He is not as strong as me, but I appreciate that he has the nerve to attempt to be. "I want you to allow the Gloomweavers back into the city. And turn a blind eye to what might happen when they are here . . . enjoying themselves."

Gloomweavers . . . That was not a part of the bargain I was expecting. The slave traders have long been banned from entering Luminael – unless they are here for an auction.

No taverns, inns, or whorehouses.

Elves are sneaky, but Gloomweavers are sadistic. Cruel. Feral. They do not have magic, but they have brute strength and a viciousness that scares even the most highly skilled Sunborne fae.

The Sunborne will despise me for letting them back in, and the Shadowkind will be used, abused, mistreated. The Gloomweavers will bring what's left of this city to ruin.

But without Alana, we will be ruined anyway.

And without this elf, I fear I will never find her.

"Very well." I take back my hand, down my whisky, and stand. "You find me my prisoners. You get your Gloomweavers back."

The elf grins widely, then wipes his hands on his tabard and rests them on his hips. "You have yourself a bargain, my lord. I'll start at sunrise."

FIVE

Alana

ONE HUNDRED YEARS AGO

My mother skims her hands over my shoulders, then begins to braid my hair. Her fingers move deftly, like feathers, barely noticeable. Everything about her is soft. She is warm sunshine, and delicate raindrops, and all the good things that exist in the world.

She is the only one who truly knows me. She sees what I am deep inside, and she is not afraid.

Unlike my father.

Unlike my brother.

Samuel glares at me from over by the fireplace. He loves me and yet he hates me because I see parts of our mother that he can't see. I anticipate her moods, and her needs, and I am more like her best friend than her child.

Because I feel it.

I also feel him.

I feel all of them, all of the time, and sometimes it is so overwhelming I think it might drive me insane.

I need to learn to shut it out, but no one can help me.

As my thoughts drift, my mother senses it and gives my hair a gentle tug. She knows when I'm becoming overwhelmed, and she does her best to ground me.

"Alana," she whispers, "how is Kayan today?"

My lips curl into a smile.

Samuel scoffs and rolls his eyes. "Those two will be wed before the year's out. Trust me," he says.

My mother tuts. "They are too young for that," she says. "No Leafborne marries before their second centennial."

"Those two will," Samuel says, standing up and stretching his wings in front of the fire. As he does, the flames crackle. He has the power to manipulate fire. A power inherited from our grandparents, and he loves to tease Kayan with it.

The two of them have been rivals since as long as I can remember. Friends but also enemies, they love to wind each other up. Love to compete.

Samuel lights a fire, Kayan extinguishes it.

Kayan fills a vase with crystal clear water, Samuel makes it boil so hot it evaporates.

All this time, they have never once gotten bored of teasing one another.

Sometimes, that makes me feel jealous. I cannot tease or play jokes with *my* powers. My powers are not coveted.

The ability to manipulate air, or fire, or water, or the seasons, or to converse with the animals . . . These are all things that others look at and say, *Wow, if only I could do that too.* Each one contains *something* that makes others jealous.

When people look at me, all they see is poison. An insidious gift that makes them feel like they should avoid me, stay away, keep me on the outskirts of the community.

My mother tries to make them include me.

But my father . . . He is perhaps the worst of them all. He does not trust me. I can tell in the way he looks at me, and in the way the air shimmers a dark, greyish blue when he is around me. He is constantly guarded, as if he doesn't care to know me at all.

And I feel as though I do not know him either.

"Shall we go for a walk?" My mother finishes braiding my hair and stands up. She takes my hand and helps me to my feet. I'm wearing the emerald green dress she sewed for my birthday last year. It reaches down to the floor and hangs in soft folds that rustle gently as I move.

I nod, unsure why she wants to leave the cabin so late at night.

But when we are outside, she takes hold of my hand. She grasps it tightly. "Alana, there are whispers in the village. People are talking about making you leave the forest."

My eyes widen and dread settles in my stomach. Leave? Where would I go?

"They intend to hold a vote. If it is successful, they will force you to leave. Go to the city." She blinks quickly, trying to stop the tears that are swelling in her eyes. "I have been refused a vote. So has your father, and your brother."

"Samuel knows about this?"

My mother shakes her head. "Not yet. He is going on his quest tomorrow. We didn't want to tell him before he left."

I shake my arms, trying to dislodge the tension that has settled inside them. I flex my fingers and pace away from her, bare feet meeting the cool soil, toes nestling in.

I have been to Luminael only once before, and I hated it. I cannot live there. It is too crowded. There are too many of them; too many thoughts, and feelings, and people, and noise. It would drive me to an early grave.

"Mother, what can I do?"

"Show them that you can control yourself." she says softly. "Change the way you talk to them, the way you are when you're around them."

I tilt my head, her fear and worry overwhelming me. "I don't know what you mean."

"That . . ." She clasps my face and stares into my eyes. "Exactly that, Alana. When you are reading my emotions, I can tell. Your face changes, you blink strangely, and your voice becomes vacant. Like you're not really there. You need to stop. You need to make them think you're no longer doing it, even if you are. You need to hide what you are. Otherwise, they will make you leave." Her voice is urgent now, higher pitched. Her eyes sparkle, wide and scared, in the dim evening light of the forest. She grabs hold of my hand and kisses my knuckles. "Please, Alana. Please promise me you'll try."

I swallow hard, crossing my arms in front of my chest. "All right, I'll try."

She leaves me like that. Walking back to the cabin, telling me she'll give me a moment to compose myself because Samuel must never know. Not before he leaves.

I lean onto the nearest tree and exhale heavily. I don't know how to do this. I don't know how to change who I am.

I WALK BACK TO THE CABIN SLOWLY, MY MOTHER'S WORDS echoing in my mind. Dread coils in my stomach at the thought of being forced to leave the forest – my home. The only place I've ever known.

But I have no idea how to be who they want me to be.

Over the next few days, I try my best to follow my mother's advice. I focus on keeping my face impassive, even as I'm bombarded by the emotions of everyone around me. Their fears, their judgements, their mistrust. When I speak, I concentrate on keeping my voice neutral and concealing any hint that I can sense what they're thinking and feeling.

But it's draining, this constant effort to hide myself from sight. By the end of each day, I'm utterly exhausted – mentally, emotionally, physically. And deep down, a sinking feeling tells me that even this won't be enough.

When the vote finally takes place, the outcome is not a surprise.

In the central square, what seems like the entire village

gathers to cast their decisions. My mother and father are present, but they are not allowed to vote.

Samuel left three days ago to start the quest that each fae must complete when they turn one hundred and fifty years old.

If he was here, what would he say? What would he do?

I stand alone, trying to hold my head high despite the hostile stares boring into me from all directions. My heart pounds as the elders collect and count the wooden voting tokens.

When they announce the results, I barely hear their words over the roaring in my ears. The verdict is nearly unanimous – I am to be banished from the village and sent to live in Luminael. Exiled.

Forever.

I am given three days to say my goodbyes and pack my belongings.

In that time, I refuse to speak to Kayan or Rosalie. They knock, and beg, and plead. But I remain completely silent.

The only way I can cope with this is if I *don't* have a tearful goodbye.

I wouldn't even know how to say goodbye to Kayan if I tried.

At sunset on the third day, there is a knock on the door. My father is sitting in the corner, pretending to focus on a book. He doesn't even look up.

My mother answers, and steps aside, tears rolling down her cheeks.

The village's strongest men and women – six of them – file inside the cabin and flank the walls. "It is time to go," Maura says.

Instantly, rough hands grab my arms on either side, and I'm jostled forward as they start to march me down the path leading out of the village. Craning my neck, I look back frantically, desperate for one final glimpse of my family. But even my mother is not watching.

We're on the outskirts of the village when I spot them.

Kayan, Rosalie, and . . . Samuel?

He is sprinting toward us, his face etched with anguish and outrage. "Stop!" he yells, drawing his sword. "Release her! You cannot do this, you have no right!"

"Did you tell him?" I call to Kayan, shaking my head. "He wasn't supposed to know."

Samuel draws to a stop in front of me. He is bigger than a lot of Leafborne fae, with dark hair and sparkling blue eyes. He flexes his wings. "Unhand my sister," he growls.

For a moment, a fragile twinge of hope blooms in my chest. Perhaps he can make them see sense.

But it is gone almost as quickly as it arrived.

My escorts try to push past him, muttering platitudes like, *The vote is cast, it cannot be undone,* and, *You will still see her. Just not here.*

"This is her home," Samuel growls.

Then his hand moves to his waist. His blade flashes in the sunlight and his eyes narrow. What is he doing?

"Let her go," he says darkly.

The hands gripping my arms simply tighten. They try to move past him, but he lunges for one of them. His knife slices through the air.

I yell for him to stop.

I beg Kayan to stop him.

I stumble back, and Rosalie is at my side now, grabbing my hand. Not afraid of me.

Tears blur my vision as I watch the guards surround my brother. He has always had a quick temper, and has rarely been able to see sense once it takes hold. But I can tell from the way he's fighting that he doesn't intend to hurt anyone. He's simply trying to stop them taking me.

But he is outnumbered, and the guards escorting me don't know him the way that I do; they don't know that he wouldn't hurt them. That he was the kind of boy who cried if a bumblebee died in our cabin or a snail was accidentally trodden on.

Samuel drops his blade and splays his fingers. Fire magic crackles in them. He raises an arm and throws fire so it surrounds me, and Rosalie, and Kayan. "If you want her, you'll have to go through me first," he shouts.

But then he stops shouting.

I scream as Samuel falls to the ground and goes still. He is clutching his chest. An arrow protrudes from the spot just above his heart.

I try to reach him, but the flames hold me in. I beg Kayan to dampen them, but he simply holds onto my waist and tries to keep me still.

Samuel turns and meets my eyes. Already, the light is fading from them. His blood stains the earth. He whispers something I can't hear, and blinks slowly. The guards are just standing there. No one is doing anything to help him.

"Why aren't you helping him?" I shout above the crackle of the flames.

As Samuel closes his eyes, the fire withers to nothing more than embers on the ground. I push Kayan away and run to Samuel's side.

He is not breathing.

My protector, my brother, is gone.

Because of me. Because of what I am.

SIX

Alana

The voice comes again in the middle of the night. Finn's arm is wrapped tightly around my waist, his body warm and comforting beside me. But when the voice comes, it makes my entire body stiffen.

I uncurl myself from Finn, trying not to wake him, and stand. I reach for my robe and wrap it around myself. Outside, it is freezing cold, but I do not stop to put on more layers. The voice is calling me. It wants me, and suddenly I know I cannot resist it even if I want to.

I walk out into the moonlight completely barefoot. The soil is like a balm for the soles of my feet, the cold nothing but comfort as I let it sink in, drifting up my calves and into my bones.

It quickly becomes a shudder, but I lean into it. I close my eyes and breathe, trying to make the voice come to me again. When it does, it whispers my name and lands like feathers of ice on my skin. I flex my fingers. As I move then, beads of condensation drift up from the grass around me, catching in the moonlight, joined by fireflies that make them glow.

The droplets are beautiful. I breathe out slowly. The voice comes again, and the water drifts up into the air, swirling around my legs and my waist. Then it tightens around me, moving faster, swirling, coiling like a snake snatching its prey.

Something nudges me. But when I try to turn, I can't.

The voice calls again, and I realise the water is telling me to follow it.

I glance back at the tent, where Finns's sleeping form is silhouetted on the canvas by the flickering light inside. He would tell me to stay with him. Or perhaps he would think I am losing my mind.

There must be a reason I haven't told him what's happening in my head.

Perhaps it's because I believe Eldrion is doing this to me.

Perhaps it's because I believe I *want* Eldrion to be doing this to me.

When the voice calls again, I lean into the sound. It is not Eldrion, I know that. And yet I cannot help seeing his face in front of me. It sends shivers of arousal and anger down my spine, zipping through my bones like splinters of smooth flint. Deadly but beautiful.

I hate him.

But I want him.

And as the water continues to swirl around me and I follow the voice into the depths of the forest, I close my eyes. I do not watch where I am going. Something is guiding me.

Is it him? Is this the moment he finally takes me? Has he come for me?

My feet remain slow, absorbing every second of contact with the forest floor. As I move, more droplets join the ones already swirling, until they are a torturous tornado, propelling me forward into the dark crevices of a forest I do not know.

I should know it.

We have been here long enough now, and yet it still feels unfamiliar. Not like home. Everything here is harsh and sharp and divided. There are fractures within us and around us.

Instead of coming together to fight, we are fighting each other.

And instead of respecting me finally because I helped them to escape, my kin hate me. They despise me. They see me with Finn and they want to throw stones at me. I can see it in their faces.

His kind – the Shadowkind – hate me too, because they think I believe I am above them, and that Finn favours me.

Once again, I have become a pariah amongst my own kind.

And maybe that is why I lean into the voice. I let it take me. I let it pull me into the murky depths of this foreign place, and teach me the steps to follow.

It whispers my name, again and again, a haunting rhythm.

Visions flash in front of my eyes. Or fire and coals and dancing. I hear the drums. I see the scene in front of me as if it were yesterday. The moon celebration. Kayan.

I see his face.

I peel my eyes open and blink into the darkness.

Something glimmers in the distance. A flicker of movement. The promise of a shadow that my eyes cannot quite catch hold of. I blink again, harder, trying to make it make sense.

This time, when I move, the water drops to the floor. It falls in a puddle at my feet, and leaves me trembling with cold.

I wrap my robe tighter around my naked body, suddenly wishing I had put on more clothes.

There it is again. Like a whisper, floating between the trees.

It moves, and with it comes a flicker of greenish blue light.

My breath halts in my ribcage. Then it swells and turns into anxiety. I reach out, trying to feel for a person. Fae, human, elf.

I am close to the shield the fae cast around our camp. I am almost at its very edge. I can feel the magic. It presses down on me and around me, and it feels both exhilarating and terrifying at the same time.

Of course, I was not one of the ones who cast the shield. I could not; I have no magic that is useful in terms of spells or incantations.

My magic is nothing but a drain on me and those around me.

And yet . . . the beads of dew on the forest floor still tremble. I can feel them. If I close my eyes, it's as if they are talking to me. And then other sounds rush to my ears, too. They drown out the voice. Rivers, waterfalls, rain on the other side of the valley. The ocean, the tide.

I stumble back, clutching my stomach as the strength of the sensations overwhelms me.

When I open my eyes, a low murmur parts my lips.

Kayan.

He is here.

I see him.

Blue lights swirl around him, like the water that swirls around me. They have become dancing fireflies, zipping up over his body, illuminating the cords of muscle on his chest and the rivets above his hips.

His wings stretch out to either side of his body, into the trees. They glow, too.

I am transfixed by him. I cannot look away. Visions of Eldrion ripping those beautiful wings from Kayan's body and throwing him over the parapet of the castle pummel my eyes. Pain racks my body, but when I open my eyes again, Kayan is smiling at me.

He reaches out his hand.

I walk towards him, and then the voice in my head changes. It solidifies. Becomes real. It is him. It was Kayan speaking to me, all this time.

I float towards him above the ground, my wings fluttering with the anticipation of being close to him again.

But then his body shimmers. Literally becomes translucent before becoming real again, and I realise it is not him. He is not here.

"Is it you"? I whisper.

He does not answer, just keeps his hand outstretched for me to come closer. I move towards him, and when I finally take his hand, the water and the lights swirl around us both, tying our limbs together.

I feel him, and yet I do not feel him. He's there but he is not there.

I shudder violently. A rush of something that feels like cold air sweeps like a tornado through my veins, wrapping around my muscles and my bones and every sinew in between.

Kayan looks down into my eyes.

"Is it you?" I whisper.

Again, he doesn't speak, but he moves closer. With his other hand, he touches my face.

His skin is darker than it was, and it does not look real. It shimmers, but it is both light and dark at the same time, like he is made of the shadows that appear at twilight.

Blue shadows.

Shadows and water.

His wings beat slowly, but no breeze touches my face.

I look down at his hand. I cannot feel him. I am imagining him. Surely?

"It is me." Finally, he speaks. He leans in close to my ear, but there is no breath. No warmth.

I find myself wishing he would slide his hand into my robe and touch me there. Anywhere. Everywhere. So I can feel him. But he does not.

"It is me," he says again.

I stare into his eyes. I recognise those eyes. I would know them anywhere, but I do not trust myself. I can't. This could be a trick. Eldrion could be doing this, he could have infected my mind.

Or perhaps the forest.

Or the Shadowkind.

Something.

Someone.

As if he can tell my thoughts are spiralling, Kayan dips his head to catch my gaze.

My god, he is beautiful like this. Was he always this beautiful? He tweaks a finger under my chin and I move as if I have felt him, even though I did not.

The water that binds our wrists continues to swirl.

Kayan turns around and leads me with him through the forest. "Water will give us both the power we need," he says calmly.

I follow like a child being led by a grownup they trust. I trust him completely, even though my mind is telling me not to. My body trusts him. My body knows him. My soul knows that this is the friend I've known for so long.

"Alana . . ." When we reach the edge of the shield, Kayan points to the lake just beyond it. "We need the water."

"I can't let down the shield. I didn't cast it." I shake my head, tears pooling in my eyes because I don't want him to leave and I feel like if we cannot reach that water, he will. He will go. And I'll never see him again.

Somewhere behind me, blue and purple butterflies drift up from the forest floor. They glow too, like the fireflies. They drift towards the shield and float right through it.

Kayan raises his eyebrows at me. "You can do anything you desire, Alana. You are stronger than you know."

I let go of his hand. The water disappears. I walk forward. The shield shimmers in front of me. I stretch out my fingers. I have seen the others do this, when they tested its strength. Every single one was met with a hardness. Like glass that they could not penetrate.

But my fingers slip right inside it, like they are sliding into a slab of melted butter. I move closer. And then I am through. On the other side, turning to look back at the part of the forest which was supposed to be protected.

If I can get through . . . can't others?

Kayan is in front of me. I did not see him cross the threshold of the force field. But he is here. His wings continue to beat slowly, but still they do not move the air.

As he walks, I look down at the damp sand at the shore of the lake.

He leaves no footprints. When I follow him, only mine lead to the water's edge.

But when Kayan does reach the water, it ripples. It remembers him and his power.

"I took your powers," I whisper.

He nods slowly, staring out at the lake. "You did."

"They've been inside me all this time."

"They have."

"And when you died . . ."

"Your emotions set you free." He turns, smiling.

Without really thinking about it, I move closer and hold out my hand. A small ball of ice forms in my palm. I skim it across the lake the way we used to skim stones, and it sends sparks of blue magic up into the air.

Kayan grins. "I knew you'd get it," he says.

I turn to him. "Is it really you?"

He nods slowly, his grin turning into a sad smile. "It is, but I am not . . ." He wrinkles his nose the way he used to when he was struggling to give me an answer about something. "I am not a living thing anymore, Alana. I am . . ."

"What? What are you?"

He fixes his gaze on the lake. "I'm not sure."

SEVEN

Finn

It's almost sunrise. The rest of the camp is sleeping. Except for Alana. She thinks I don't know that she sneaks out before sunrise to walk alone. That she enjoys the hours when everything is quiet.

But I know her better than she knows herself.

"What's with the long face?" Yarrow asks, plonking down next to me.

I don't meet his eyes, just sigh and grit my teeth. "We've been here so many weeks, it is actually starting to feel like home. Honestly, though, I expected the Shadowkind to be a little more grateful; we are free of Eldrion. Those of us who dared, at least. For the first time in centuries, for some of us, we are free."

"Except, we're not, are we?" Yarrow yawns, sloshing coffee into a cup and sitting down hard on a log by the campfire. He scratches his beard and turns to look at me.

Instead of sitting, I pace up and down in front of the fire, wings twitching. "What do you mean?"

Yarrow chuckles and shakes his head. "Look around, Finn. We've taken them from one prison to another. We can't leave the forest, can't go beyond the boundary of the protection shield. Which – I might add – we wouldn't have if it weren't for that old Leafborne fae. Maya . . ."

"Maura," I correct him.

"Which is making the Shadowkind uneasy. Plus there's no real plan." He taps his foot. "*Is* there a plan? Because, for years, we've talked about the day we finally escape and plot our revenge. And now it seems like all we're doing is playing house in the forest, listening to you fuck your Leafborne girlfriend."

I bite back the urge to tell Yarrow that last night was the first time in weeks that Alana and I had been intimate with each other. That being here has damaged what we built when we were each other's salvation back in the castle. That, so many times, I thought I was losing her.

I look down into my coffee. It's strange that it took her telling me she'd been with someone else – Eldrion of all people – to bring us back together.

But fate works in strange ways.

"I have been waiting for news from the elves. You know that."

"Which elves?" Yarrow isn't going to let me get away with half answers anymore.

"I have contacts. They were supposed to be reaching out to

the Shadowkind that remain the Luminael, finding out who will join us when the time comes."

"But you have heard nothing. It has been weeks. I'd say it's time for a new plan, wouldn't you?" Yarrow folds his arms in front of his large chest.

He's right. The elves were always a risk, but it was a calculated one. I figured using them for intel was a better bet than trying to send one of us into the city, and risking being caught.

"We need them." Yarrow taps his foot again. "If the plan is still to destroy Eldrion, we need more numbers." He gestures to the ramshackle tents that have been set up around the clearing. "The Leafborne can't be trusted. I don't believe they'll join us in a fight. Last time, we caught Eldrion off guard and we were running. Not fighting. Next time . . ."

"It's not just him." I stop and sit down next to Yarrow, then meet his eyes. "I want to take down all of them."

Yarrow studies me a moment, then laughs loudly. When my expression doesn't change, he breathes out hard and pinches his nose. "Fuck, Finn. What you're saying . . ."

"I want to kill every last Sunborne in that wretched city. Destroying Eldrion isn't enough. He'll go, someone else will take his place. But if we kill them all . . ." I lower my voice and lean in closer. "Yarrow, if we kill them all, we really will be free. Finally. Free."

There is a long, heavy pause, then Yarrow rests his forearms on his knees and stares into the fire. "You don't have to ask me twice to go and kill a load of Sunborne," he says, smirking a little. "But *how?*"

"We'll need to strike hard and fast." I pick up a stick and begin to sketch in the dirt in front of us. "The tunnels remain our best bet for entering, especially as they collapsed. If we can find a way back through, then target the barracks, the armoury, and the throne room simultaneously, we'll cut off Eldrion's access to reinforcements. Obviously, and this is where the elves were supposed to be doing their bit, we need numbers. We need to know for sure if Eldrion has replaced us or if he's operating on a skeleton staff."

Yarrow shakes his head, laughing a little. "He's an arrogant bastard. He won't have replaced us. As far as he's concerned, we just want our freedom. To spend our days playing in the sun like every other free fae. Wouldn't occur to him that we'd come back for him."

"I agree. But I'd still like proof." I pinch the bridge of my nose. I've been avoiding leaving the safety of the forest, and our protection shield, but I'm being left with very few options, and time is getting away from us. "I'll go to the city. Today. Track down the elf who was supposed to be helping us. Get answers. Then we'll know what we're dealing with."

I half expect Yarrow to tell me not to be so foolish, but he doesn't. "All right," he says. Then he makes a dismissive gesture with his hand. "So, say we get our answers from the elves. The castle is up for grabs. The Shadowkind of the city are willing to join us."

I nod along, waiting for what's next.

"You're forgetting something."

I frown at him.

"They have magic. We don't. And the Leafborne sure as hellfire won't help us if they think it'll be a risk to them." Yarrow flicks his wings, and visibly bites back the urge to sigh. "Forget Eldrion, the Sunborne themselves are powerful. The most powerful fae in the kingdom. You don't think they'll fight back?"

My nose twitches. My jaw, too. I trust Yarrow. More than I trust any other fae here. If this is going to work, I will need his help.

A slow smile spreads across my face as I straighten up. "That, my friend . . ." I glance towards my tent. "Is where Alana comes in."

EIGHT

Eldrion

It has been at least half a century since I thought about my mother, really thought about her. But since the night in the tavern, I have not been able to rid her from my mind.

Perhaps it was the way the patrons talked about me. He's losing it. He's past it. Rebellion.

She never said those things to me. She never told me she was disappointed in me or that she wished my brother hadn't died when he did.

But I could see it in her eyes when she looked at me. As clear as day. She longed for him, not me. She believed the family's gift died with him.

I am standing on the roof, staring out at the sunrise. Usually, I prefer sunset because it brings with it the shadows I find comforting, but today I decided to try and remind myself what it is I'm fighting for.

Early, like this, with the sea glistening under the sun's warm orange glow, and the rooftops of Luminael slowly being brought back into the world of colour, the city is almost beautiful.

I am reminded of the days when gold-tipped spires glistened, and music rung out in the streets.

The days before I drove it to ruin in an effort to save it from itself.

The visions began soon after my mother died. As she was lowered into the family tomb, beside my father and my brother, something shifted inside me. I felt it. Like my bones were creaking and trying to bend, like my skull was too tight for my mind.

My wings itched to stretch and be free and soar over the city, even though I was told as a child that flying like that was a foolish pastime.

Something the frivolous Leafborne practised.

Not us.

Not the Sunborne.

I ignored the sensations, drowning them with whisky. I pretended they were not there, or that they were some form of grief, and that any moment I'd wake from the haze of my loss and feel able to rule the way I was supposed to.

They did not disappear.

They intensified.

The first vision almost broke me. It was one of the most vicious, visceral visions I've ever had. Even now, two hundred years later, I remember how it felt.

So real, so tangible. I woke convinced it had already happened; that the city had gone to ruin and everyone who lived in Luminael had been swallowed by darkness and fire and flood.

As I realised what had happened, something else settled in my core. Deep. So deep it has remained there for two centuries, digging in, gnawing, scratching.

I knew, after that vision, that something was coming to end us. Something within the city. Something no one could see or feel. Something that was creeping in plain sight.

I knew I had to control it, contain it, watch the city like the cruel overlord they expected me to be so that the moment the evil revealed itself, I would be there to stop it.

Two centuries. I still don't know what's coming.

All I can hold on to, the only true thing I know, is that Alana is important.

I started seeing her face soon after that first vision, and she was so different to the others that she drew me in without even trying.

My nightmares brought me darkness, and pain. Anguish and terror.

And then there was her . . . Porcelain skin, freckles on her nose, hair the colour of autumn. She was a light in the darkness, and yet despite the comfort she brought me, I did not trust her.

I craved her, and I loathed her. Because I wanted to believe she was the key to my salvation, and knowing how much I wanted it made me think she could be the opposite. She could be the one to end it all.

What if this woman, this ethereal fae with sea-green eyes and fire in her soul, is a temptress sent to bring me down?

What if she is not fae, but demon?

I stare out at the citadel, the water, the forests in the distance and the mountains beyond. She is out there somewhere, and she is too far away. Every fibre of my being needs her closer, craves her, desires her.

And yet, I hate what she has with the Leafborne boy. I almost obeyed her. For a flickering fraction of a moment, I almost let him live because I did not want to see the despair in her eyes.

When she fucked me in the tunnels, I could have captured her, brought her back here.

I could have dragged her here, kicking and screaming and naked.

But I needed her.

I hate how much I need her.

I hate that my heart beats with the rhythm of her name, and that I whisper her name when I am alone and the darkness is threatening to overwhelm me.

"Eldrion . . ."

A voice, like ice laced with poison, drips down my spine and settles in the crevices between them. My wings are outstretched, hiding the silhouette of the voice's owner. But I know with absolute certainty exactly whose face I will see when I turn around.

"Mother," I whisper.

A hand touches my shoulder. I turn my head. There she is. Piercing silver eyes, ochre skin, long silver hair tied in braids that cascade down her back.

She smiles, and for perhaps the first time in my memory, it feels like a true smile.

"You're not real."

She sits down on the parapet and crosses one leg over the other, as if we are meeting in a tavern for drinks and feasting.

"What makes you say that?" She tilts her head.

"I see the future. I do not see spirits."

"You saw the future. You did not see spirits." She taps her fingers on her thigh. She's wearing the dress she was buried in, a silver gown that looks like the shimmering surface of the ocean when she moves. "Things can change, Eldrion."

"Have you changed? Do you still hate me, Mother?" I stare ahead at the sunrise, but I can feel her watching me.

"I never hated you." She stands and takes my hands. "I was scared for you."

I look down and flex my fingers. I can't feel her. She's not here. My mind is playing tricks on me.

"I was terrified, after your brother died, that you'd be left all alone without the power to rule." She touches my chin, turns my face towards her.

"Your fears were well founded," I reply.

But, to my surprise, she shakes her head. "You are wrong, son. You have exactly what you need. You just haven't realised it yet."

"I have destroyed this city because I wasn't equipped to interpret my visions. They are not complete, like yours were. And I am no prophet, like Raylon. I see snippets of what the future holds, but I can't make sense of them." I turn to stare out at the city. "Look at what I have done in the name of keeping these people safe. I have destroyed Luminael, and I have lost myself. My heart is black and wizened. I hate everything, and everyone –"

"And yet you still try to keep them safe . . . You search for the empath because you know she is important."

My wings twitch at the mention of Alana. "You know about her?"

My mother inclines her head. "I have always known about her."

"How?"

A slow smile parts my mother's lips. "I know her, son, because I created her."

Tar-like dread sweeps over me. My mind is playing tricks. This is not real. It cannot be real.

"What do you mean, you created her?"

"She is not what you think she is."

"What does that mean?" Shadows start to swirl around my feet. My fingers splay out to the side, my wings block out the light of the rising sun. I am taller than my mother, and stronger. I tower above her, but she does not quake or seem afraid. "Tell me what you mean!" I reach for her. Grab her. Try to catch hold of her wrist, but my hand goes right through her.

She is not there.

"She is not what you think she is," my mother's voice whispers.

"Wait . . . stop." I spin around, desperately searching for her. The shadows grow thicker and darker, they grip my ankles, my legs, they spread outward, over the parapet, down the sides of the castle. The sunrise quivers and darkens.

And then it starts all over again.

The screaming.

The demons.

The death.

The end.

I wake on the floor of my chamber. I don't know if I was ever on the roof or if the whole thing was a dream. It is becoming harder to tell the difference between waking and sleeping, reality and nightmares.

I stagger to my feet, grabbing hold of the mantle above the fireplace.

I pick up my whisky glass and draw it to my lips. But instead of drinking, I throw it into the fire.

The glass shatters and crackles.

The flames burn brighter.

And then the voice comes to me again. "She is not what she seems."

NINE

Alana

When I touch Kayan's hand, a spark, like static, zips up my fingers into my wrist. Up my arm.

What *is* he?

He is here, and yet not here. Tangible, but just out of reach. The urge to wrap my arms around him, to feel his solid warmth against me is almost unbearable.

I lost him, and now he's back, and to not be able to hold him is like torture.

"Kayan," I whisper. "What do you remember?"

He tilts his head. His movements are slow, fluid, like water moving over pebbles in a stream.

"I remember *him*." His voice darkens. "Eldrion. He looked into my eyes . . . Right into them. Then he . . ." He blinks, a calmness washing over him.

He tilts his head, brow furrowed in concentration as if trying to grasp an answer that eludes him. "I died."

"Yes." Tears are flowing down my cheeks now, but I can't stop them. I don't even try. "You did."

As I watch Kayan visibly trying to piece together the missing fragments of his life, and death, I pause. Then I let down my gates. I search his entire body, but find nothing.

I have never felt anything like it before.

He is like a void, a silent, welcoming void.

I sigh and brush my hands through my hair. I don't know if he's really here, or if my mind is slowly descending into madness. But I know how I feel; for the first time in weeks I feel at peace.

I lean closer to the silence and wait for him to be able to speak.

"It's hard to explain, Alana. I feel . . . different. Not quite whole."

I reach out tentatively, my fingers passing once again through the glimmering outline of his hand. "Do you know why you are here? With me?"

Kayan reaches down and touches his index finger to the water's surface. Small blue lights dance out from his fingertip.

He doesn't answer me, but when I dip my finger into the water, too, and the same thing happens, he smiles.

"You have my magic," he says.

I nod, wanting so badly to touch him as I tell him this. "I think I took it from you when we . . ." I trail off, blushing even though it's ridiculous to blush when talking to a ghost. "It's been inside me all this time. Grieving for you unlocked it."

"So, that's how your powers work." Kayan smiles and reaches out to stroke my hair from my face. A sensation, like the memory of a breeze, caresses my cheek.

"I steal from people," I mutter uncomfortably.

"No." He shakes his head. "Well, yes. But only when powered by emotion. Right?"

"I can take their pain and their powers," I whisper.

Kayan dips his head to meet my eyes. His shine like moonstones in the night.

"I helped the Leafborne when they were grieving for you. I took their pain away."

"Like you did for your mother after Samuel died."

I frown at him. "Samuel?" The name snags somewhere beneath my ribs. I have not thought about my brother for years. I cannot. It still hurts too much.

"Don't you remember? When she stood by his grave and —"

"Don't." I turn away, striding back to the shore as the water splashes around my legs. "I can't talk about him."

When I reach the shallow waters, Kayan is suddenly in front of me again. He seems larger than before. Brighter. More beautiful.

"Then let's talk about something else," he says, tilting his head from side to side as if his thoughts are finally clearing.

"I think I am here to guide you, Alana. I think there's something you need to do, something important. But I can't . . ." He trails off.

"Can't what?" I press gently.

He shakes his head. "I can't tell you why, or what it is. The knowledge is there, just out of reach. Like a word on the tip of my tongue."

"So, you came back to play cryptic puzzles with me? To distract me from how awful this situation is?" I laugh.

Kayan frowns, then smiles slowly. "Perhaps it will become clear on its own."

"Perhaps," I repeat, sitting down on the sandy earth by the lake and tucking my knees up under my chin.

When Kayan sits beside me, his wings flutter. They are back to how they were before I destroyed them, and before Eldrion tore them from him. Except they are even bigger now, and brighter.

"I miss you," I whisper. "I wish I could hug you, just one more time."

Kayan's smile is tinged with sorrow. "Me too. More than anything." He moves closer, his form shimmering. "But I'm here. We got more time together. We have to be grateful for that, don't we?"

Tears prick at the corners of my eyes. But beneath the pain, a flicker of warmth settles below my heart. He is with me still, in whatever form fate has allowed.

I square my shoulders and lace my fingers together. "Then we'll figure this out together. Whatever I'm meant to do, whatever you're here to show me. We'll figure it out."

Kayan nods, his eyes shining.

"It's nice to have a true friend beside me again," I whisper, picking up a stick and tracing circles in the earth.

"You have Briony and Finn," Kayan says, staring out at the lake. "Are they not true friends?"

His question feels different from the other words that have crossed his lips.

Briony and Finn.

"You don't think they are my friends?" I turn and try to meet his eyes.

Slowly, Kayan turns to look at me, too. "I can only help you find your own answers, Alana. I cannot give them to you."

I narrow my eyes at him, then try to laugh, attempting to dislodge the unease that is congealing in my stomach. "Cryptic Kayan is going to be heaps of fun," I mumble.

He laughs too, but as we sink into comfortable silence, I cannot ignore the ball of unease that has settled in my chest.

Briony and *Finn*?

Finn . . .

He loves me. He would never hurt me.

And Briony is my best friend.

I can trust them.

Can't I?

TEN

Alana

ONE HUNDRED YEARS AGO

We are gathered under the light of the moon. The lake glistens, her surface dancing with the caress of the pale yellow light that filters down from a starry sky.

Any other night, it would be beautiful.

Tonight, it is the ugliest moon I have ever seen.

I am standing at the back of the crowd that has gathered by the lake. Kayan appears beside me and takes my hand. He squeezes it hard, and leans down to press his forehead against mine. "I'm sorry," he whispers.

Rosalie is at my other side now, and she too grabs my hand. "I'm sorry, too, Alana."

I cannot answer them. Grief hangs so thick in the air I can barely breathe. Mine, my parents', my friends'.

Gathered together on the eastern side of the lake are the fae who killed my brother. The ones who were escorting me from the village when he tried to stop them.

They have not been punished, or stripped of their ability to use weapons, or banished from our village.

There have been no consequences except having to face the destruction in my mother's eyes when they broke the news to her.

My father stands by the moon rock, wings tucked neatly behind him. The ethereal green glow that denotes his connection to the earth is more muted than usual. He does not search for me or try to seek my gaze.

Next to him, my mother is mute and wears the expression of someone so lost in her own sadness she might never return. She doesn't look for me either, but it is not because she hates me.

It is because she loves me, and she has lost me.

In the morning, I am to leave. Despite what happened, the villagers were unanimous; Samuel's death only served to prove that I am a danger to the Leafborne. When was the last time one of us died prematurely? When was the last time we held a funeral for a fae of Samuel's age?

Has there ever been a fae death so young?

With Kayan and Rosalie beside me, I try to ground myself. I try to shut out the tidal waves of pain that barrel towards me, and threaten to overwhelm me.

But it is too difficult.

Their pain merges with mine and grows bigger, stronger, more consuming. Until I can barely breathe, barely see.

I pull out of Kayan's grasp and turn away from the lake. As the ceremony starts, and my brother's body is pushed out to the centre of the lake by the elders with water magic, I stumble towards the treeline.

In the darkness of the forest, away from the clearing and the sight of the fire fae lighting torches that will turn Samuel's body to ash, I sink down to my knees and bury my face in my hands.

Maura is the one who finds me. I know her presence immediately and look up from my palms to see her skinny legs and wizened hands.

She crouches in front of me and tilts her head. "You are to stay," she mutters.

I can't speak.

"Did you hear me? You are to stay, Alana." She stands, not an ounce of sympathy showing in her words or her thoughts.

"Why?" I blink up at her through tear-filled eyes.

"Because your mother is a good woman, and she will not survive losing two children." Maura extends a hand to help me to my feet. My wings flutter a little as I straighten myself. From the ground nearby, a purple butterfly floats up into the sky, then disappears behind a clutch of bushes.

"Thank you." I wipe my cheek with the back of my hand.

Maura looks me up and down, purses her lips, then sighs. "I truly wish you had never been brought into this world," she says. "It was foolish." She shakes her head, then turns away from me. "Foolish fae," she mutters as she walks away. "Foolish fae."

ELEVEN

Finn

I have not set foot in Luminael for over a century. The last time was a rare exception. A day pass to accompany the chef to the market because her usual kitchen assistant was unwell.

Until the night we escaped, I spent my entire life in Eldrion's castle, watching Luminael from the parapets after dark, or early in the morning. Observing the Sunborne aristocracy in their finery.

I had forgotten that there were less well-off Sunborne in the city. Of course, they still consider themselves better than us lowly Shadowkind – and their magic is still stronger – but they are not all as pristine and proper as those who attend Eldrion's banquets.

The elves do not usually mix with the Sunborne. They are the ones who run the taverns, and the markets. They have their own quarter of the city and associate mainly with other elves. They are the keepers of secrets. They know everything and reveal nothing. Unless they feel it will be to their advantage. And, even then, the advantage must be great.

I met Garratt when he came to the castle to deliver ale for one of Eldrion's feasts. We ended up sitting on some haybales in the courtyard, drinking some of his own private stash, and discussing all manner of things. Largely, why none of us ever dared to just get up and walk out of the castle.

I remember laughing and twitching my wings at him so my piercings jingled. "We cannot walk out, he'd hear us."

"So?" Garrat asked me, taking off his cap to reveal a shock of white-blond hair and the traditionally pointed elven ears. "You think he'd kill every single one of you? He'd have no one left. He wouldn't do that."

"Easy for you to say. Elves are a free people. You have never been subjected to what the Shadowkind have . . ."

"True," Garratt said, scratching his chin and lighting his pipe. "That's true."

After that, as the ale grew warmer and our tongues looser, we came to an arrangement: if it ever became possible for the Shadowkind to escape, the elves would be on our side.

"We're not fighters, mind," Garratt said, chewing the end of his pipe. "But we will keep watch for you."

"Why?" I narrowed my eyes at him.

Garratt shrugged and raised his eyebrows. "Because I believe you're destined for more than performing party tricks for the fae lord. And I'd like you to be in my debt." He grinned and puffed on the pipe. "It's always beneficial for someone in power to owe you a favour."

Now, as his words echo in my head, I remember the way I felt in that moment. Like something shifted deep inside me. I'd always dreamed of escape. We'd been plotting our 'rebellion' for years. Centuries. The tunnels were a legend among the Shadowkind of the castle. But it was only then that I started to believe it could happen. And that I should be the one to lead it.

I don't know why that elf made me think differently.

I've thought about it many times since.

Perhaps because they are so wise, so all-knowing, and he saw something in me.

Perhaps because fate whispered in my ear that he was someone I could trust.

Now, though, I'm starting to wonder if fate got it wrong.

It has been weeks since I heard from Garratt. When we first escaped from the castle, I sent word via raven that we would be in touch, and asked him to keep his word and keep his ear to the ground. *Send the bird back when you have news, he will know where to find us.*

I have watched the shield every day. Paced the perimeter looking for the raven, and found nothing.

So, either Garratt changed his mind, or something else is happening in the city. Something to prevent him helping us.

Our first meeting at the castle was fifty years ago. We have been friends ever since, drinking together regularly when he brought ale to the castle. I refuse to believe he has changed his mind.

Which means . . .

I pull my cloak up higher around my face. I'm sticking to the shadows, trying to slip through the market crowds of the elven quarter unnoticed. More than anything, I'm trying to keep my wings completely still. Because if anyone catches my bells on the breeze, this could all be over.

As I approach Garratt's inn, I pause and assess the doors and windows. It's early morning. The inn is locked up tight, and won't be opening until midday.

Do I wait? Or do I knock?

Instead of rapping my knuckles on the front door, I head around back to the stable yard where patrons tether their horses. I slip into the shadows and quietly tap on the back door, the one that leads into the kitchen, then remain as unnoticeable as possible until the door finally creaks open and a familiar blond head peers out into the sunny yard.

"Who's there?" Garratt grunts, pinching his nose.

I wait, making sure he's alone, then slip past him into the kitchen. I am lithe, and fast, and my movements are like water. I am perched on the countertop, swinging my legs back and forth when he closes the door, bolts it, and turns around.

"Holy mother of . . ." Garratt slams his hand against his chest. Then, slowly, a grin spreads over his face. He rushes over, claps my shoulder. "It is very good to see you, my friend."

I lean back against the countertop, my brow furrowed, the momentary pleasure at seeing my friend fading as I remember why I'm here – and what I've risked to be here.

"Garratt, I've been waiting for word from you. Why haven't you been in touch?"

Garratt's grin fades, too, replaced by a more sombre expression. "I'm sorry, my friend. There was nothing to share until yesterday."

"Yesterday?"

"Something happened that you need to know about."

I stop swinging my legs and lean forward onto my thighs. "What is it?"

"I had a visitor." Garratt raises his eyebrows at me. "Lord Eldrion himself came to my inn."

This time, I sit up straight. A bolt of anger lodges itself deep in my throat at the mention of Eldrion's name. "Here? Eldrion was here?"

Garratt nods slowly. "He's looking for the Shadowkind and Alana. Killed and tortured an elf for information."

"Do the other elves know where we are?"

Shrugging, Garratt shakes his head. "Doubtful, and if they did, they wouldn't give up that information. Even when tortured. Unless Eldrion had something to offer them in return. And, by all accounts, he's not thinking too clearly of late."

"He's not?"

Garratt leans back on the counter opposite and takes his pipe from his pocket. He taps his temple with his free hand. "Losing it," he whispers. Then he laughs, "As proved by the fact that he wants *my h*elp to find them."

"He asked for your help?" I'm not sure whether to laugh or be worried.

Biting his pipe, Garratt says, "I offered it. In exchange . . ." He bites back a chuckle. "In exchange for Eldrion letting me form some sort of elven police. Letting me run the elven quarters as I see fit. Invite the Gloomweavers back into the city."

"Why would you want to –" I stop myself from asking the question. I don't care what Garratt's motives are, only whether he is still on my side or if he's now indebted to Eldrion.

As if he can read my mind, he says, "Don't worry, I have no intention of handing you over to him. I want Eldrion gone from the throne as much as you do."

My body relaxes a little, my wings twitching behind me.

Garratt chuckles, a sly smile playing at the corners of his mouth. "But I told him I'd be more than happy to assist in his search. Even offered to put my best elves on the job."

"If he finds out you're playing him."

"He won't." Garratt glances at the door. "As long as you don't hang around here too long." He pauses, then adds, "Eldrion has no friends in this city. The Sunborne are afraid he's losing control. They're keeping themselves to themselves. The Shadowkind are either plotting to join you when they can, or they're in complete denial. Still serving their masters as if nothing has happened."

"Even those still in the castle?" I cross my legs now and extend my hand to ask for a puff on Garratt's pipe.

"Most. There are a couple who wish they'd joined you. They might be useful when the time comes."

"You think the time is soon?"

Garratt nods. "Right now, Eldrion is distracted by his obsession with the empath. You should strike soon if you truly intend to."

I begin to pace the kitchen, my mind racing. If Eldrion is truly unravelling, if his grip on power is slipping, then Garratt could be right. No more hiding in the forest like cowards; this could be the perfect time to finally fan the flames of rebellion and bring the Sunborne to their knees.

"Garratt," I say, turning to face my friend. "I need you to keep playing along with Eldrion. Feed him false leads, keep him distracted. The more time we have to plan and gather our forces, the better."

Garratt nods, a fierce determination in his eyes. "Consider it done. I'll send word again in a few days, let you know what else I've learned. But Finn . . . don't hang around. If Eldrion was his usual self, I would be advising you to run. Not fight."

"Thank you," I say, clasping Garratt's hand in a firm shake. "I can't tell you how much this means to me. To all of us."

Garratt meets my eyes. "It's time, Finn," he says, his voice low and intense. "Time for the Shadowkind to rise up and take back what's theirs. As long as you remember it was the elves who helped you get there when you're sitting on the throne in Eldrion's castle."

TWELVE

Kayan

My body is not my body. It looks like mine, but it's brighter. Bluer. It glistens and small shivers run through me every time I move.

The things that happen, happen without me having to think about them. Moving, appearing, disappearing.

I knew Alana was going to be in the woods. I was nowhere, and then I was there with her.

I am here and I am not here. I know what I'm here to do. I know how much I can show her, and what I'm not allowed to show her. Yet, no one has explained the rules.

It is just there. Knowledge, that feels eternal, like I've never not known it.

As the sun climbs higher in the sky, Alana leads me to the edge of the lake once more. The water is still, a perfect mirror reflecting the endless blue above. I hover beside her, my ethereal form shimmering in the golden light.

"I want to show you something," Alana says, a glint of excitement in her eyes. "Something I've been practicing."

I tilt my head, curiosity piqued.

She grins, a mischievous expression that I know all too well. "You'll see. Just watch."

With that, she turns towards the lake, confident and sure. The Alana I remember. The woman I fell in love with so many years ago. Before she was just my friend. Before Rosalie.

I try to shift thoughts of Rosalie from my mind, direct them back to Alana. She is my purpose here. She is my reason for returning.

I watch as she closes her eyes, her brow furrowing in concentration. For a moment, nothing happens.

And then, I feel it. A surge of power, a ripple beneath the surface of the lake. The water crackles with energy, and I swear I can taste the magic on my tongue.

Alana's eyes snap open, and she raises her hands, palms outward. The water begins to churn, a whirlpool forming at the centre of the lake. It spins faster and faster, a vortex of liquid fury that sends spray flying in all directions.

But that's just the beginning. As I watch in awe, the waterfall at the far end of the lake begins to slow, then it stops altogether. The roaring cascade hangs suspended in mid-air, droplets glittering like diamonds in the sunlight.

And then, as I stare in disbelief, the water begins to flow backwards. It rises up the cliff face, defying gravity, defying the rules of science, and bending instead to Alana's will. To her magic.

I turn to stare at her, transfixed more by the expression on her face than by the magic itself.

Her features are a picture of fierce concentration, her eyes shining so bright it's like a fire burns inside her. Her purple wings are spread wide, catching the light, and for a moment, she looks like a goddess.

The reversed waterfall reaches the top of the cliff and begins to spill over the other side, creating a new cascade that flows away from the lake. It's a sight that takes my breath away, a display of raw power and skill that I never could have imagined; she doesn't just have my power, she has *supercharged* my power.

Finally, with a flick of her wrist, Alana releases her hold on the water. The whirlpool dissipates, and the waterfall resumes its normal course.

She turns to me, her chest heaving, her face flushed, her freckles brighter than usual, her eyes sparkling.

"Well?" she asks, a grin spreading across her face. "What do you think?"

I shake my head, lost for words. "Alana, that was . . . incredible. I've never seen anything like it. I've never *done* anything like it. How did you . . .?"

She laughs and shakes her head, and something tells me it's the first time she's laughed like that in a long time. "I'm not sure," she says. "I haven't practised since we left the castle. I thought it was the adrenaline of the escape that powered the magic. But maybe . . ." She looks down at her fingers. "Maybe it's just there now. Whenever I need it."

I drift closer to her, my own essence buzzing with the after-glow of her power.

"Do you mind?" she whispers, her smile dropping. "I took this from you." She flexes her fingers.

I shake my head. "Never. I could never mind," I chuckle.

Alana's smile softens, and she reaches out instinctively, her fingers passing through my translucent form.

"You wear them better than me," I tell her, nodding out towards the lake. "Power looks good on you."

"I hope you're not flirting with me," she says, her cheek dimpling. "I'm taken."

"By Finn?" I try not to let my tone become gravelly at the mention of his name. Try not to let her see how uneasy I feel at the thought of him. At all of the Shadowkind.

She nods, studying my expression. Is she trying to read me right now? If she is, she'll have no luck.

"I'm taken, too," I remind her, sitting down even though I have no need to. "At least, I was."

Alana swallows hard. "Do you know what happened to her?"

I shake my head. "Do you?"

She smooths her hands over her skirt and wriggles her toes into the damp earth. "No. The last time I saw Rosalie was at the auction." She sighs, hard, the joy she was feeling a moment ago waning. "You can't find out where she is?"

I sigh, too, even though the feeling I want to feel is like the ghost. Not quite there. Not quite tangible. Muted.

"It doesn't work like that." I beat my wings slowly, causing a soft breeze to drift over us.

Alana laughs, this time a softer, sadder laugh. “I wish you could tell me exactly how it did work,” she says.

“Trust me.” I meet her eyes. “So do I.”

THIRTEEN

Rosalie

I have stopped counting the days I have been locked away here, and I have stopped thinking about the others.

All except Kayan.

And Alana.

I hope that, wherever they are, they are at least together. Is it strange that I hope that? Knowing their feelings for one another could quite possibly be reignited if they were to endure the kind of torture I have endured.

I look around my chambers. Of course, to the outside observer, this does not look like a prison. I have a large, comfortable bed, a wardrobe full of fine clothes, and a view of the lawns.

But fear and loathing hang in the air here. It is thick with them.

No one speaks to me except *him*, and I do not know if that

is because he has commanded it to be that way or because they are simply too afraid.

I have tried to make friends with my maid – the Shadowkind woman who comes to dress me each morning. But she refuses to meet my eyes.

Once, she touched the cuff on my wrist. For a brief moment, hope bloomed in my chest and I thought perhaps she knew a way to take it off so I might escape. But maybe she was just curious.

She has never done it again, and still has not uttered a single word.

Not even when I am naked and she is shampooing my hair in the bath, or when she turns down the sheets at night. Not when I am crying, or shouting, or pleading.

I gave up a few weeks ago.

At least, I think it was a few weeks ago.

I have given up counting the days.

I glance over at the mirror, then stand and turn it around. On the back, I had begun to etch the number of nights I was kept here. I stopped counting when I reached forty.

I trace the markings with my neatly manicured nail, and sigh as I turn the mirror back around. To think, there was a time when I longed to be a Sunborne aristocrat. It began after a visit to the city for a parade. My mother took me, and I was instantly entranced by their beauty and their power.

Now, I have all the trappings I wanted. But they come at a price.

Thinking of my husband, bile rises in my throat.

I did not agree to the marriage, but apparently that does not matter when you are a Sunborne marrying a fae you have purchased at auction. He simply nodded when the priest asked him if he wanted me as his wife, and that was it.

A gold band was slipped onto my finger. And I was his. Officially.

Tonight, there is to be a feast. I have heard the servants muttering about it. They quiet when they know I am close by, so I have perfected the art of sticking to the shadows.

The garden is the best place for this. I can linger behind a hedge or fountain and catch snatches of what the gardeners are saying to one another.

This feast, in particular, is important because my husband is trying to impress the Sunborne who *usually* attend gatherings at the castle. I have heard talk of Lord Eldrion. Something about him losing some servants and cancelling the festivities that usually happen on a nightly basis in the citadel.

My husband clearly believes he can obtain favour with some important people by stepping in to fill the void.

The sound of my bedroom door opening makes me quickly pace away from the mirror and stand, hands clutched in front of me, head bowed. In case it is him.

I recognise the feet at once. It is not my husband but my maid.

I sigh and look up. But today, for the first time, she meets my eyes. She clears her throat. "My lady," she says.

Her voice is shocking. Not because there is anything wrong with it, but because it has been so very silent within these walls for so long now.

"Your husband requests that you join him and his guests for the banquet tonight. They are not to know how you came to be his wife. If you are asked, you will reply, 'I should let my dear husband tell you that story.'" She is speaking like she is reading from a script. Her words are stilted, and once again she is struggling to look at me.

"Will you not have a real conversation with me?" I duck my head to meet her eyes. "Please. Just one word of sincerity."

I don't know why I think it might work this time; every other time I've tried to talk to her, she has refused. She ignored my tears, why would she listen now?

"What do you want to talk about?" The question stuns me. I blink at her for a moment, then grin and rush forward, throwing my arms around her neck.

"I'd like to know your name." I take her hands between mine and squeeze. "Please. Tell me your name."

"Terra." The maid dips her head into a nod. "My name is Terra. But now I have to go. I will return to dress you for tonight."

As Terra leaves, my heart soars.

She has a name, and she gave it to me. Which means I have a chance – just a small chance – of getting her to be my friend.

I know how pathetic that sounds. But it is so lonely here.

I have never known a loneliness like it, and if I have to endure it much longer, it might just break me.

Trying not to think about the evening's approaching events, instead I cross back to the dresser. From the drawer beneath the mirror, I take out a small piece of paper. It is a page ripped from a book that I was given when I first arrived. Next, I take the eyeliner that formed part of my makeup casket.

I look down at the sketch I started a few days ago. It is not quite right yet, but I will capture his likeness.

I close my eyes, summoning Kayan's face to my mind. Then I open it and start to draw. When I have finished, I will draw Alana, too. Maybe even Samuel, although it has been so long since I thought of him, I'm not sure whether I'd be able to conjure his face anymore.

I bite my lower lip, trying to concentrate. But my eyes are blurring with tears.

I push the paper away, stand up, and go to the bed. I lie down, burying my face in the pillow, and begin to cry.

"Please, come and get me," I whisper. I am not sure if I'm speaking to Alana or Kayan or both of them, but I know I need to pray to someone. "Please . . . don't forget me. Don't leave me here."

FOURTEEN

Alana

Finn has been missing all day, and I'm almost glad of it. I have only just gotten over keeping one secret from him, and now I have another to hold close to my chest.

Except, this one feels even more dangerous. Because who would believe that I am talking to a ghost? If I told Finn I was seeing Kayan's spirit, and that we'd had a conversation, laughed, done magic together, talked for hours while the sun slowly rose, would he believe me?

I'm afraid he'd think I'd lost my mind.

I'm afraid I might be losing my mind.

First, the visions and the vivid dreams about Eldrion – a man I despise, but who can make me come in my sleep when he's not even touching me. Now, this.

I have heard of fae communing with spirits. But I always thought they were rumours or tales to amuse children with, perhaps to comfort those who've lost someone. I never expected them to be true. And I certainly didn't expect the spirit world to have such a strange, confusing set of rules.

Kayan tried to explain as best he could. But he doesn't seem to understand, either. All he knows is that he was alive, then dead, and now he's somewhere in between. And that he is here to 'guide' me, not 'tell' me what to do.

As much as I hate being told what to do, I can't help but wish the spirits were a little more lenient in this regard. It is all I can do to keep my grip on reality; trying to interpret signs and signals from a ghost might prove a little too much to handle.

Kayan disappeared when the camp started to wake up.

I both long for him to return, and long for him not to.

Seeing him was glorious, but it was also hard because it forced me to remember how it felt to lose him.

I feel exhausted and the day has only just begun.

When I spot Briony talking with a group of Shadowkind, I wait patiently for her to finish and then wave to her. She heads in my direction, collecting coffee from the ration station on her way. "You look like you need this," she says. "Are you all right?"

Instead of answering her, I nod in the direction of the Shadowkind, who are still muttering amongst themselves. "What's going on?"

Since we arrived, the two factions of our camp have been divided, but matters have been getting worse over the past few days.

"They are not happy with Finn. He's disappeared again,

except this time Yarrow has promised he will return with information."

"Information?"

Briony sips her coffee and shrugs. "Something to help us make a plan."

I sigh and pinch my nose. I should be more concerned about what Finn is planning, but the visions haunting my dreams have distracted me from reality. "I thought escaping was the plan?" I ask, sitting down on the log by the fire because my legs are starting to ache with tiredness.

"It was." Briony nods. "But there was always a bigger plan, too."

I tilt my head. This is the first I've heard of there being *more* to the Shadowkind's escape. "Bigger?"

Briony sighs a little. "I shouldn't be telling you this," she mutters. As she speaks, Kayan's words filter back into my head. But how could he possibly suggest I shouldn't trust her? She's sharing things with me. See? She's my friend.

Unless she is manipulating me and what she's about to say is not true.

I try to push the thoughts from my mind. As I do, I'm certain I see Kayan's shadow flickering in the distance. Beyond the fire.

I ignore it.

"Finn has always talked about overthrowing Eldrion," she sighs. "Honestly, I thought that it was all bluster. That as soon as we escaped, he'd realise we're better off running as far away from Luminael as possible. But . . ." She looks worried now, her eyes wide, her small wings rustling nervously. "Yarrow is a bad influence," she says, grimacing. "He is reckless. And he hates the Sunborne."

"As should you," Finn's voice interrupts us from behind, making me jump to my feet, wings fluttering, purple light trickling outward and fizzling away into the air.

Briony stands slowly.

Finn tilts his head and folds his arms in front of his chest. "Do you not hate them, Briony? For what they have done to us?" He makes a show of fluttering his tattered wings. The chime of the bells both arouses me, because it reminds me of all those times he was between my legs or inside me, and makes me shudder. Because of what they mean.

"Finn, you know I will always support you. It's just . . . we're free. Shouldn't we –"

"You call this freedom?" Finn's voice rises in volume, and a look crosses his face that I haven't seen before. I want to slip my hand into his and calm him down, but something tells me my involvement won't be welcome.

With a flourish, Finn strides to the centre of the clearing and claps his hands. "Everyone," he calls. "Gather around. Leafborne, Shadowkind . . . everyone."

Yarrow looks up from where he was sitting whittling an arrowhead out of wood, then stands slowly and is the first to join Finn by the fire.

Slowly, the others join, too.

Gathered with the Leafborne, Maura barely looks at me. Hatred swells around her every time she is near me or Finn or the Shadowkind.

I wish I could find a way to make her remember that moment in the cellar. When I helped them all. *You took away their grief.* Kayan is beside me. I can feel him. *I see it now, Alana,* he says. *Why didn't you tell me? It was magnificent. You are . . .*

I shake my head, trying to dislodge his voice from my consciousness so I can listen to what Finn is saying.

Don't just listen to their words, Kayan mutters. And then he is gone.

Is he talking about Finn? Or Briony? Perhaps Yarrow?

How am I supposed to know when my mind is already so confused?

"It is time we discussed our next steps." Like this, Finn looks masterful. No longer the court jester but a worthy leader. The past few days, his energy has waned, but now, the spark in his eyes is back.

He puts his hands on his hips and stares out at the others.

"We are not free," he says, glaring at Briony. "We are out of the castle, but we are still living under Eldrion's shadow. Confined to these woods. Unable to leave for fear of being recaptured. By him. By Gloomweavers."

A murmur of agreement goes around in both groups of fae. At last, the Leafborne and the Shadowkind agree on something.

"Even if we flee from here, we will never be free. Look at what happened to the Leafborne . . ." He turns to them, his voice softening. "You were captured, torn from your village, and brought to the castle. And there is not a corner of the kingdom far enough away that Eldrion couldn't reach us if he wanted to. Unless we live under a protection shield for the rest of our days. Locked in a leafy green cage instead of a stone one."

"So what do you suggest?" It is Maura who speaks, crossing her arms and striding forward. "What do you plan, jester?"

"Before I tell you what I plan . . . I need to show you something. All of you." Finn's entire stance has stiffened. His body is coiled tight, fists clenched at his sides. He strides toward the fire. "We all know that the Shadowkind have long been repressed by the Sunborne."

"And that all other fae have turned a blind eye to it because it doesn't affect them," Yarrow adds darkly, looking at the Leafborne.

Pen jerks forward as if he's about to object to Yarrow's words, but Maura puts her hand out to stop him. "Let them speak," she says calmly, assessing them with her glimmering eyes as her wings beat slowly behind her.

At her feet, the ground glows green. A warning? Or a coincidence? The earth responding to her emotions? Or a hint that Finn needs to be careful not to forget that the Leafborne are the only ones here with any actual magic.

Ignoring her, Finn strides towards the fire and reaches into his pocket. "I want to show you all something," he says. "Because I am afraid we have all forgotten the atrocities our ancestors suffered at the hands of Lord Eldrion and his family. In fact, at the hands of *all* Sunborne. For generations. For centuries."

The crowd goes quiet. I move a little closer to Briony.

Beyond the fire, I'm certain I see Kayan's blue shadow moving amongst the Leafborne. Watching, listening.

What is Finn doing?

I try to catch his gaze, to look for reassurance, but he does not look in my direction. Instead, he begins to pace up and down.

"I think some of us here need to be reminded exactly how bad things have been and could be again. For we have been living in relatively peaceful times. Eldrion uses his strength now and then to scare us into submission, but largely we have been left unharmed as long as we do as we are commanded to do."

A trickle of ice-like fear drips down my spine, spreading through my body. Although my gates are closed, the unease radiating from both groups of fae presses up against them, knocking, pounding, demanding to be let in.

Finn takes something from his pocket. It looks like a small, velvet bag. He opens the neck and dips in his hand, then spins towards the fire and throws in a handful of dust.

It blooms purple, bright, white, then deep, then the flames jump higher.

A tidal wave of heat hits my face. I jolt backwards, and so do the others, but Finn tells us to come closer.

"Look into the flames," he commands. Above us, despite it still being daylight, the sky is darkening. "Look into the flames and concentrate on what you see. Remember it. Absorb it. For *this* is the reason we must rid ourselves of Eldrion and his kind. *This* is the reason running away and hiding will not save us."

The sky darkens further. Storm clouds gather, and a crack of purple lightning forks down towards us. It catches a tree, and the branches immediately catch light. A murmur passes round the group. Fearful mutterings. A water fae steps forward to dampen the flames, but Finn shakes his head.

"Wait," he says.

The flames turn to smoke. Deep purple smoke that drifts down from the tree and creeps across the ground. It grips my ankles. It is warm and cold at the same time, sending needle-like pricks of discomfort up towards my knees, my thighs, my hips.

I stretch out my arms. The smoke is enveloping all of me now. I look for Briony. She is gone. All I see is smoke and, flickering behind it in the distance, Kayan's blue light.

I try to move towards him, but my feet will not budge. I am stuck to the spot.

And then it starts.

Screaming.

So loud it makes me slam my hands over my ears and screw my eyes shut. It is a scream full of anguish, and dismay, like a body breaking from the inside out. Over and over and over again.

When I open my eyes, I am standing in a field. But it is not daylight. It is dark. The moon shines brightly.

In front of me, a group of young fae. Perhaps fifteen, sixteen years old. Wide-eyed. Practically babies, even though they think they are adults.

They hold hands, shaking, trembling.

Their attire is not like ours. It is older, reminiscent of that I've seen in textbooks that detail our culture from the dawn of the fae, through the golden ages, up to now.

Another comes into view. This fae, however, is not a child. She has silvery hair and piercing, emerald eyes. She paces up and down in front of them. Then she clicks her fingers.

A group of Sunborne – I know they are Sunborne because of their ethereal complexions and their enormous wings – step up from behind her and form a line. One by one, they approach the shaking young fae.

I study their faces. Their wings are small, but all fae of that age have small wings. We do not develop our adult wings until we are fifty years old, and it is only then that our powers fully bloom.

But there is something about them; the wide eyes, the sallow skin, the fear.

They are Shadowkind.

The fae pacing towards them hold ropes. Not the kind Finn used in his displays in court, or the kind we used when we played with each other's pleasure.

These ropes are solid, metal, silver perhaps.

The first fae to fall to their knees is a girl. Long red hair, freckles. She could be me.

She begins to cry silent tears as the ropes are wrapped around her, her wings pressed so tightly against her small body that I can see the metal digging into her delicate skin.

She sobs, screams, wails. Then the others start. The sounds bring nausea to my throat.

The scene changes.

We are in a large wooden cabin, a dormitory perhaps. The girl is trying to free herself from the ropes. She is struggling so hard that her skin is becoming red raw and inflamed.

Things change again. She is older now. The rope is still tight. Her wings have drooped, lost their colour. She looks broken.

She takes a knife.

She brings it to her wing.

"No," I whisper. "Don't do that . . . don't do that to yourself."

She hesitates, then she throws the knife to the ground and pummels the nearest tree with her fists.

After that, a million other images pummel my brain.

A young fae boy lies curled on the ground, his wings bent at an unnatural angle. His sobs echo through the air, pure, unadulterated agony.

A Shadowkind woman, her belly swollen with child, is held down by Sunborne guards. A hooded figure approaches, a glinting blade in hand, and begins to cut away at her wings, even as she screams and begs for mercy.

I want to look away, but I am frozen, trapped. Tears stream down my face, my heart shattering inside my chest.

Finally, mercifully, the visions begin to fade. The smoke dissipates. We are back in the clearing. Everyone is weeping. Only Maura is dry-eyed, but she turns away and walks to a nearby tree, bracing her hand on its trunk and breathing slowly. Using the earth to ground her.

Finn steps forward, his own eyes red-rimmed and haunted. "Do you see now?" he asks. "Do you remember what they did to us?"

The Shadowkind answer as one. "Yes," they whisper almost in unison. "We remember."

Finn turns to the Leafborne. He stalks toward them. "And you," he says. "Will you stand with us in our fight, or will you turn a blind eye like you have always done?"

For a moment, there is silence. The Leafborne look terrified. Not one of them glances in my direction.

But then, to my surprise, Maura turns around and slowly steps forward. She draws herself up to her full height, her green-tinged wings flaring out behind her.

"We will stand with you," she says.

"Maura . . ." Pen speaks up, but she hushes him immediately.

"For too long, we have been complicit in the suffering of the Shadowkind. We have looked the other way, telling ourselves that it was not our fight, not our problem."

She looks around at her fellow Leafborne, her eyes blazing. "But no more. They helped us escape. Now we will help them."

For a moment, there is complete silence. Then Pen sighs heavily, looks around at the others, and purposefully steps forward. "Tell us what you need us to do."

FIFTEEN

Eldrion

My skull is pounding. Lightning rods of pain ricochet around my head. With each stab, her face appears.

Alana.

My mother.

Alana.

My mother.

Then Raylon too.

We were so alike we could have been twins. That's what everyone said. Except, I knew different because he had the power I did not. And he had our mother's love.

He was lucky, until he was not.

The screams begin, and then the voice. "She is not what she seems. I created her. She is not what she seems."

My wings flail out sideways and something clatters to the floor, shattering on the cold flagstones.

"My lord?" A voice I don't recognise. A figure appears. A tall, broad shadow. Small wings.

"Why are you still here?" I pry my eyes open and glare at the silhouette. It folds its arms and shrugs.

I blink harder. Female. Dark hair. Red lips. Is she real?

I jump from the bed and cross the room in seconds. My hand is around her throat. Her eyes widen. I take my blade from my waist and press it to her cheek. I press hard enough to make her bleed. Then I bring the crimson droplet to my mouth and taste it.

I feel her heart beating close to my chest. Fear congeals in the air around her.

I step back, sheathe the knife, and find my robe.

"I am still here because I have nowhere else to go," she says.

"What is your name?" I narrow my eyes at her.

"Pria," she replies. "My mother was your mother's handmaiden."

"But you are a guard?"

"I am."

"Do you intend to kill me, Pria?" I sit down, legs open. I'm wearing pants, but I notice her gaze drop to my crotch.

She does not blush. "No. I intend to serve you. It is what my family were born to do. I have no desire to change the way of things." She shrugs and adjusts her sword.

"Would you fuck me if I asked you to?" I lean forward onto my knees. As I speak, Alana's face fills my vision. I blink her away. Maybe I can fuck her out of my system.

Pria shrugs. "I'm sure you'd be a good fuck, my lord. I am open to the suggestion."

I stand and stride back over to her, sling my arm around her waist, and grab her chin with my other hand. But when my lips meet hers, a taste like bile fills my mouth.

I stumble backwards and shake my head.

"My lord?" Pria narrows her eyes at me.

She does not taste like Alana. Nothing is as sweet as Alana. "Leave." I point to the door and stalk away, back to the bed.

"I will, my lord, of course. But I came to tell you there are elves in the courtyard, and they say you are expecting them."

I stop, back to her, and try to fight the fury that rises in my gut. It's no use. The shadows show themselves. They begin to slink out from beneath the bed, turning to smoke, weaving around my legs and up towards my waist. My eyes darken. When I turn around, Pria is shaking.

Now, she is afraid.

Good. If she was lying and intended to stab me in my sleep, maybe this will make her think twice.

"Take me to the elves," I command in a timbre three octaves lower than usual. "Now."

In the courtyard, Garratt is sitting on top of a bale of hay, kicking his feet as if he is on a longed-for vacation. He looks up, pipe between his teeth, and grins. "Ah, Lord Eldrion." When he jumps down, he sweeps into an exaggerated bow.

He spots the shadows at my feet and swallows hard.

All around the courtyard, silence descends. The Sunborne who are part of my inner court and were out here enjoying the fine weather are staring. A couple cling on to each other, looping arms and looking terrified.

The remaining Shadowkind in my employ slink back. Afraid. Quaking in their boots.

Garratt bites his lower lip. He's afraid, but he's also cocky.

"I have an update for you, my lord. Perhaps we should go inside?" he asks, tilting his head. Behind him, two more elves wait for my response.

I turn and motion for him to follow me.

In the grand hall, I slam the doors closed, shouting for Pria to make sure they are guarded.

From the ceiling, the remnants of Finn's last performance hang like ghosts. Rustling in the breeze that comes through the broken window. Damn that jester. Damn him. If he knew how important Alana was, would he have taken her from me? Would he have hidden her away if he knew she was the key to our salvation?

Garratt stops and puts his hands in his pockets. "I've been asking around," he says. "No one has seen your fae."

"That is what you came here for?" I stride towards him,

ready to end him right here, this second. And his friends, too.

He holds up his hands, palms out, in defence. "No, I came to ask about your visions."

My body stiffens, dread coiling in my veins. "Visions?"

Garratt raises his eyebrows. "Servants talk. They say you are losing your grip on reality. Your mother had visions, did she not? And your brother before he died?"

"No one knew about them. How do you know?" I thrust my hand around his neck and squeeze. Every fibre in my body wants to squeeze the life from his useless little throat.

He coughs. One of the other elves speaks up. "We know most things," she says. "Elves have always paid attention to the things fae are too busy to notice."

I blink hard, trying to stay present, trying not to think of Alana.

I loosen my grip.

Garratt rubs his throat as he steps back a few paces. "Elodie is right," he says. "If the fae had ever bothered to pay attention to us, they'd know that we are more powerful than they think. Because our power lies in knowledge."

"Stop talking in riddles, elf. What is your point?" I flex my fingers as the shadows begin to twitch in my peripheral vision.

"My point, Lord Eldrion, is just that if you need help interpreting these visions . . . I know somewhere you can go. And I can tell you how to get there." Garratt's lips stretch into a smirk. "For a fair price, of course."

SIXTEEN

Alana

"Finn . . ." I catch his elbow as he stalks away into the cover of the trees. It's approaching nightfall. He was gone all day and didn't tell us where he went that prompted such a decisive change in his demeanour.

"Finn . . ." I repeat myself, fluttering in front of him to block his path.

He glowers at me. His body is taut with adrenaline. Like a tiger that needs to kill a deer in order to expel the bloodlust from its body.

It was the vision. Of course, it was.

While it embedded sadness deep into my bones, and the bones of the others, for some it left simply rage.

Molten rage.

As if he can't control it any longer, Finn turns and slams his fist into a nearby tree. He is panting, his wings fluttering, the bells chiming.

I put my hand on his shoulder, then his wing. I trace the tips, gently, softly.

His breathing slows.

"How did you do it?" I ask, leaning forward to kiss the soft underside of his wing tip.

Finn sighs and puts his palms flat on the tree trunk. His knuckles are red and sore. He presses his forehead to the trunk as I continue to kiss him, because it is the only thing I can think of to bring him back down to himself.

"The vision." I wrap my arms around his waist and slide one hand just beneath his waistband. "How did you do it, Finn?"

"The elves gave me the spell." He is muttering, lost in the feel of my touch and my kiss.

"Elves?" I frown, caught between questioning him further and paying attention to the warmth building between my thighs.

Finn mumbles an agreement. "They are going to help us. They hate Eldrion as much as we do." He looks at me over his shoulder, then. "You do hate him, don't you, Alana? I know he infected your mind, but you see what he is?"

I swallow hard. A rush of arousal beats a hard pulse in my core at the mention of the fae lord's name. And I hate myself for it more than I hate him.

"I always hated him. I always knew what he was. You have to believe me, Finn –"

Finn turns around, grabs me, and switches positions, so that I'm pressed up against the tree. "I believe you," he breathes, planting delicate kisses on my throat, then allowing his teeth to gently graze my skin. "I believe you will do whatever it takes to help us."

I sigh into his touch and spread my legs as his hand finds my wetness. He touches me for only a second before pushing my underwear aside, pulling down his pants, and driving his cock into me.

My eyes widen as he slams my hands up above my head.

He keeps my gaze, arousal swimming in his eyes.

Holding onto me, as I wrap my legs around him, he fucks me hard and fast. The energy flowing from his body to mine drives me wild. He cups my face with his hand, kisses me hard, and fucks me so hard my back and wings scrape against the tree trunk, leaving claw marks of bark that will still be sore tomorrow.

When he hooks his fingers into my mouth and tells me to suck them, I moan onto his hand. He tilts his pelvis, and finds the spot that drives me wild.

I have wrapped my arms around him, and my legs, and I'm crying out as pleasure threatens to swallow me whole, when my vision blurs.

"Good girl, come for me while he fucks you."

It's him. His voice. In my head.

Is he watching me?

My eyes fly open, but I can't stop the sensations rolling down my spine, curling in my limbs, making my skin flush and my legs shake.

"Come for me like a good little fae."

I look at Finn. I don't know if it was him speaking or if I heard the voice in my head.

"I'm going to come for you," I breathe through gasps that nearly drown out my words.

Finn's eyes flash wider. "Come for me, Alana."

"You too." I cup his face with my hands and stare into his eyes. I want to watch him come, I want to stare at him like this so I know he is here and I am with him and that we love each other.

No matter what.

He grabs hold of my waist as if he cannot get close enough to me or far enough inside me. "Fuck," he breathes, still holding my gaze with his.

My wings start to flutter against the bark. It is rough. It scratches and threatens to tear their thin, fragile fibres. But I don't care. I would bleed for him. I would die for him.

"Good girl . . ."

As the voice overwhelms me once more, a volcano of hatred erupts from my chest. "I want him dead," I cry, eyes boring into Finn's so he knows I'm telling him the truth. "I want him out of my head, and out of this world. For good."

Finn grins at me, then kisses me with a passion I've never felt before. His tongue searches for mine, he nibbles my lower lip, and then he cries out, "Come with me, Alana. Come with me."

My back arches. My wings beat against the bark. My legs tremble. I tilt my head back and call his name as an orgasm spreads in tsunami-like waves through my body.

When Finn comes, too, it is hard and quick. I feel him grow harder and bigger inside me. His body stiffens. He yells, and holds onto me tight, pressing his forehead against mine as he fills me up.

As we come down from our high, sweat-laced bodies pressed against one another, panting, holding hands, he whispers, "Did you mean it?"

I meet his gaze.

"Will you really help me kill Eldrion?"

I brush my thumb across his lips. "Yes," I whisper. "I meant it. I want him gone, Finn. Gone from our lives. Forever."

As we stand there, our bodies still intertwined, Finn's expression grows serious. He brushes a strand of hair from my face.

"Alana," he says, his voice low and urgent. "There's something I need to tell you. Something important. If you're going to be a part of this, I want to be honest with you. You need to know everything."

I frown, a flicker of unease stirring in my gut. Kayan's words echo in my head. *Don't trust what they say.*

"What is it?"

He takes a deep breath, as if steeling himself for what he's about to say. "My plan . . . it's not just about taking down Eldrion. It's bigger than that."

I tilt my head. "What do you mean?"

"I want to destroy all the Sunborne," he says, the words tumbling out in a rush as excitement glistens in his eyes. "I want to reinstate equality in Luminael, in the entire kingdom. No more oppression, no more suffering. A fresh start for all fae."

For a moment, I'm speechless. The sheer scale of his ambition takes my breath away. To not just overthrow a tyrant, but to upend the entire social order . . . it's a task that seems almost impossible. Especially for a race of fae with no magic.

"Finn," I whisper, my heart swelling with a mixture of admiration and fear. "That's . . . that's a lot."

He nods, determination burning in his gaze. "We have to, Alana. We can't just remove one piece of the puzzle and expect everything to change. We need to tear down the whole damn system and build something new in its place."

I bite my lip. "But how?" I ask tentatively. "The Sunborne are so powerful, and we . . . we don't have any magic of our own."

Finn smiles then, a smile that's equal parts reassuring and mischievous. "That's where you're wrong. We have the elves on our side, and the Leafborne, and you."

"Me?"

Finn grasps my hands. "Perhaps Kayan's death wasn't in vain. Perhaps everything that happened was to allow your powers – his powers – to be set free so you can help us." He squeezes tighter, kissing my forehead. "Think of what you did when you got us out of there, Alana. The others might not see it, but I do. You saved us. We'd never have survived the tunnels if it wasn't for you."

I step back from him, adjusting my clothes. "And what of the elves?" I ask, my mind swimming as I try to picture myself coming head-to-head with Eldrion again. "They have always been neutral, always stayed out of fae politics."

"Not anymore," Finn says. "Don't get me wrong, they are completely self-interested. They aren't helping us because they believe in our cause, merely because they want positions of power in the new order."

Order. Power.

These are not words that sit well with me. They make me feel . . . uneasy.

Finn stalks over to me, fastening his belt, then leans in close, his forehead pressing against mine. "The elves, and you, and the Leafborne. Plus the Shadowkind's determination and will to fight." He grins at me. "We've got this. We can do this."

I close my eyes, letting his words wash over me. The idea of it, the sheer audacity of his plan, is both terrifying and exhilarating. To be part of something so much bigger than myself, to fight not just for my own freedom, but for the freedom of all fae . . .

"How do you know we can trust them?" I ask, my voice barely above a whisper. "The elves, I mean. How do you know they won't betray us?"

Maybe that is who Kayan was talking about. Don't trust *them.*

"They've already shared knowledge with me, spells and incantations that I never even knew existed. They want this just as much as we do."

He squeezes my hands. "I know it's a lot to take in. I know it seems impossible. But Alana, we have to try. And now is the time. While Eldrion is . . ." He trails off.

I open my eyes. "What? What is Eldrion doing?"

Finn shakes his head. "I don't want to scare you."

"Do not patronise me, Finn. You can't want me as your star player in this battle, then refuse to share information with me. Especially if it's concerning me."

Finn's lips twitch into a smile. "I love it when you're forceful," he says playfully. When I do not smile back, he adds, through gritted teeth, "Eldrion is looking for you, Alana. The elves tell me he's obsessed. He can think of nothing other than stealing you back." Finn's eyes darken. "I think he knew all along what you were capable of." He scratches his chin and begins to pace up and down. "I think that's why he had me follow you, why he bought you at auction. Because he knew what you were. Because he wanted your power."

"My power?"

"Think about it . . ." Finn is speaking quickly now. "If he could somehow have access to your powers, and learn to absorb the power of other fae, he could destroy everyone. The Leafborne, the Mountainside fae . . . He could have complete control over the entire kingdom."

As Finn speaks, my blood runs cold. I lace my fingers together and squeeze until my knuckles whiten with the pressure.

Perhaps this is what Eldrion is trying to do in the dreams he sends me. Perhaps this is his way of trying to infiltrate my mind.

"He will never have me," I snap. "Never."

Finn meets my gaze. "So, I can count on you? You're with us?"

I square my shoulders and tilt my chin. A glimmer of the way I felt in those tunnels, and when I bent the waterfall to my will, and took away the Leafborne's pain, flickers in my stomach.

"Lord Eldrion has no idea who he's up against," I say darkly. "And he has no idea what he's about to lose."

SEVENTEEN

Eldrion

The sun hangs low on the horizon, decorating the shoreline with shades of orange and violet. The pale shade of purple does not possess the vibrancy of Alana's wings. But it makes me think of her all the same. And that makes me ride harder.

Beneath me, the horse's hooves pound rhythmically on the sand. A drumbeat that matches the pulsing in my temples.

The elf was very clear. He had no map, told me none exists, but that everything is held in the memory of him and his kin.

As he spoke, I felt like a fool. How have these creatures, with all this knowledge, existed under my nose all these years?

"There is a library," Garratt said, in his usual flippant tone of voice. "It holds many ancient texts. Things the elves kept safe when fae tried to destroy them or lose them. Records we, ourselves, have kept." He shrugged and lit his pipe. "Our ancestors used to guard it. Keeping it was an honour. A duty."

"Not anymore?" I asked, frowning as my wings flicked out sideways, causing him to startle.

"No," he replied. "Not anymore. What can I say? Traditions get lost. People change."

Garratt's words replay in my mind as I ride. The salty sea breeze whips through my hair and catches the underside of my wings.

The farther I ride from the citadel, the more the weight of my responsibilities seems to lift from my shoulders. Out here, with nothing but the vast expanse of the ocean and the endless stretch of sand, I can almost pretend that I am not the Lord of Luminael, that the fate of an entire kingdom does not rest upon my weary shoulders.

But the illusion is fleeting, shattered by the relentless thump thump thump in my skull and the haunting whispers of my mother's voice. *She is not what she seems. I created her.*

I grit my teeth.

Alana Leafborne.

Garratt promised me the abandoned library would provide answers. Perhaps a younger, wiser version of me would have questioned him further or made him accompany me. But something deep inside me knew he was telling the truth. The rest of me? Well, the rest of me doesn't care if I'm marching into danger.

I would risk death if it offered an end to the questions that torment me.

I ride until sundown.

As the sun dips below the horizon, I spot the entrance to the cave, just as Garratt described. A yawning expanse of darkness nestled between two towering cliffs, its edges worn smooth by centuries of wind and waves.

I have not ventured this far since I was a fledgling fae. Perhaps I never ventured this far away from the citadel. If I did, the cave does not trigger a memory or any sense of recognition.

I dismount, my boots sinking into the soft sand. Tethering the horse to a nearby outcropping of rock, I run a hand along his glossy neck, feeling the heat of his skin beneath my palm. "Wait for me," I murmur, pressing my forehead to his. "I won't be long."

With a final pat, I turn towards the cave, my heart hammering against my ribs. The shadows seem to writhe and twist before me, calling me, beckoning me towards them.

I should find shadows comforting. I alone can control them.

But in my visions, it is the shadows that terrify me the most. And so, now, I notice a sense of cold unease taking hold of my body.

I take a deep breath, steeling myself, and step into the darkness.

The air is cool and damp, the sound of my footsteps swallowed by the heavy silence. I summon a ball of light to my palm, casting an eerie glow on the rough-hewn walls. The passage winds deeper into the earth, the temperature dropping with each step.

Just when I'm beginning to wonder if I really was a fool to trust the elf, I emerge into a vast cavern, its ceiling lost in shadows, and in the centre of the space lies a still, dark pool, its surface as smooth as glass.

I approach the edge, peering into the inky depths.

It is as black as tar.

"The entrance to the library lies beneath the surface," Garratt had said. "It won't be easy for you. Fae aren't known for their strength as swimmers."

I hesitate, but then I think of Alana, of the way her face haunts my every waking moment, and the way my mother's cryptic words echo in my dreams.

I need answers, and I have run out of places to seek them.

This is my last chance.

With a final, steadying breath, I extinguish the light in my palm and dive into the pool, tucking my wings against my back and diving down, down, down.

The water is shockingly cold, stealing the breath from my lungs. I kick downwards, propelling myself towards the bottom, my eyes straining to see through the gloom.

As I swim, a strange sensation washes over me, as if I am being pulled forwards by an unseen force. Something begins to glow, pulsing with a purple light that grows brighter and brighter until it fills my entire vision.

I squeeze my eyes shut, disoriented, and when I open them again, I find myself in a completely different place.

I am standing in the centre of a vast, circular room. The entire place glows with the same purple light, although it is impossible to tell where the light is coming from. Its walls are lined with towering bookshelves that stretch up into the shadows above, and the air is thick not with the scent of sea water but with the smell of aged parchment.

My clothes are completely dry.

As I walk, my boots tap gently on the tiled floor. I look down. It is a mosaic of coloured tiles. Smooth, beautiful.

Something about this place reminds me of the way the citadel used to be. Before my brother died, and my mother died, and I was left in charge of Luminael.

If the truth about Alana is here in these walls, perhaps I will find other truths too. The reason for Raylon's death. The reason my powers did not manifest in their full strength until long after both he and my mother were gone.

As I move deeper into the library, the air grows heavier but cooler at the same time.

I scan the shelves, but inhale deeply and let my instincts guide me, my fingers trailing along the spines of the books, until I find myself standing before a small, unassuming volume bound in deep blue leather.

Something about it calls to me, a tug in the depths of my soul that I cannot ignore.

I lift the book from its resting place and carry it to a nearby table.

For a place that is no longer cared for, it surprises me that there are not layers of dust covering every surface. But it is as if the library is immune to such things.

Everything is pristine, and perfect.

I stare down at the book. I do not know what made me choose this one, only that as soon as I touched it, it felt familiar.

The cover is embossed with a symbol I don't recognise, a twisting knot of silver that gleams in the dim light.

I trace it with my fingers, then open the book.

I scan the words, frowning, then laugh. They are completely meaningless, a jumble of ancient elven script that I cannot decipher.

Of course, Garratt sent me on a fool's errand.

I slam the cover closed and turn away from the book, but as I whirl back past the shelves, towards the pool which will take me away from here, something clatters to the floor behind me.

I turn slowly, poised to call to the shadows if I have to.

A small black book lies on the floor.

I stoop and pick it up. As soon as I flip open the cover, I recognise the ink; it is the shade my mother used to write with. Deep violet. Like the petals of an iris. And that is *her* handwriting.

I start to read, and quickly find myself needing to sit down.

I lower myself to the floor and lean against a nearby pillar.

It is a journal. The pages are filled with my mother's thoughts, her fears, and her desperate search for a way to save Luminael from the destruction that haunted her visions.

Her visions sound exactly like mine.

She writes of the darkness that threatens to engulf the kingdom, of the ancient evil that stirs in the shadows, waiting to be unleashed.

She writes of her fear for me because my powers had not yet emerged, and because Raylon was supposed to be the one to save us all. She writes nothing of his death or how she feels about it.

For that, I am thankful.

And then, I find it. The passage that changes everything.

I have seen the face of our salvation, my mother writes, her words leaping off the page with startling clarity. *A child, born of a healer's womb, with the power to turn the tide against the coming darkness.*

My breath catches in my throat.

I read the entry ten times, committing it to my memory.

As soon as I saw the child, I knew who she belonged to.

Magdalena. The healer who came to me from the Leafborne clan after Raylon's death. She came unasked, and I remember wondering why someone would do such a thing. Make such a long journey out of pure kindness.

She spent days with me, making tinctures and singing me lullabies. She was kinder to me than I ever remember my own mother being.

Now I know it was fate who brought her to me.

Now I know why we spent so many hours talking, with her counselling me through my grief.

It was all for this. So the child growing in her belly could save us all.

Bile rises in my throat as I read the next passage, my fingers clenching the edges of the book so tightly that my knuckles turn white.

I did not want to hurt her. Magdalena was sweet and kind, and clearly longed for the child she carried. But I did what I had to do. What fate had asked of me.

I found an ancient spell, a ritual of dark magic that would change the child forever, mould her into the weapon we so desperately need. The elves held the spell, of course. In their library. The price for taking it was one I am not willing to put on record.

I do not want it remembered.

But I do want a record of what I did to Magdalena. In case I was wrong.

In case, instead of saving us all, I condemned us.

Would you like to know how I did it? If you're reading this, I assume you would. Either because things have gone horribly wrong or horribly right.

It was easy, really.

I am the Lady of Luminael. Everything comes easily to me.

She had not visited for a while, but I sent word that I'd like to see her before her baby was born. She arrived, belly full and round, wearing a yellow headscarf and carrying a bunch of poppies.

I remember thinking how quaint it was that she would bring a lady a bunch of flowers.

I sniffed them, and put them in a vase.

She seemed pleased that I liked her offering.

After our usual talk and walk around the grounds of the citadel, I suggested we retire to my study for tea.

And that is when I drugged her.

She didn't suspect a thing, and didn't notice the strange taste or colour of the water. She just drank and talked, hand constantly resting on her belly.

When she finally passed out, I took the empty cup from her fingers and set it down on the table.

Then, as she slept, I performed the ritual.

A drop of my blood.

A bead of my sweat.

I mixed them with the powder the spell dictated, then I filled a large glass syringe and injected it into the child growing within her womb. With this magic, and the dark words of the incantation, I shaped her and twisted her, until she was no longer a mere fae, but something more. Something extraordinary.

I created a magic that had never before been seen in our lands. Not like this.

I created an empath, born to absorb the magic of others, to wield it as her own.

The one who will save us from what is coming.

Alana.

I knew her name because Varia had already used it. She knew her daughter's name long before she was born. And she loved her long before, too.

I whispered that name as Magdalena left that day, completely unaware that everything had changed for both her and her child.

Magdalena's child, Magdalena's flesh and blood, but my creation. My hope.

The words swim before my eyes.

Did Raylon know what my mother did? I flip the pages, desperately searching for his name, but the rest are blank.

That is all the book contains.

My mother gave Alana her powers. She quite literally *made* Alana what she is because she believed she would fight the darkness that threatens to destroy us.

Alana and her mother were nothing more than pawns in her game.

I close the book, my hands shaking, my mind reeling

I have an answer. I know what Alana is now. But it has done nothing to end my torment because now, more than ever, I know my one chance of saving us all is to bring Alana back to me.

EIGHTEEN

Finn

TWO DAYS LATER

The door groans as I enter the tavern. It is early morning, the stench of ale and smoke thick in the air from the night before. In the corner of the room, Garratt lounges in a large armchair smoking his pipe. A smirk plays on his lips when he spots me.

"Finn," he drawls. "I wasn't expecting you."

"It has been two days, Garratt. What news?" I stride over to him, boots slapping the sticky wooden boards.

I slide into the seat opposite him, leaning in, the rough wood of the table scratching my palms. "What have you learned, Garratt? Are we to strike now? What news of Eldrion?"

Garratt assesses me for a moment, looking me up and down with a slight frown on his face. "You've changed," he says. "Your energy has shifted, Finn."

"Because I'm ready to finally –"

The elf holds up his hand and shakes his head at me. "Urgency will get you killed. Time is of the essence, but so is forethought. If you don't do this properly, you won't succeed."

My jaw twitches. I like Garratt. I need his help. But he is not the one in charge, and he is not as wise and all-knowing as he likes to think he is.

He takes a long, slow drag from his pipe, smoke curling from his nostrils. Then he says, "I sent Eldrion on a little quest." His eyes shine, and he drums his fingers on the arm of the chair.

"A quest?" I sit back, fold one leg over the other, and steeple my fingers while I wait for him to continue.

"Have you ever heard of the Elven Archives?" Garratt tilts his head.

"Never."

He shrugs. "Of course, you haven't. It is ancient, full of carefully guarded secrets. But it is not meant for fae. It has been kept away from you for a reason."

"Why reveal it now?" I fold my arms in front of my stomach.

"Because I thought it might further your cause if Eldrion's mind slips a little further into oblivion." Garratt grins. "The truths he discovers there will play havoc with his already fragile mind."

"What truths?" I lean forward now, staring at Garratt with a look I hope he interprets as menacing.

"Not part of our deal, Finn. I can't share that information with you."

"Garratt, if you're playing games –"

Garratt holds up his hands and shakes his head, chewing on his pipe. "I can't because it's forbidden. Even I refuse to break the laws of my kin. No elf can share the secrets held by the library." He removes the pipe and bites his lip instead. "I can, however, tell you how to reach it."

As he meets my eyes, Garratt quirks an eyebrow at me.

"Is it worth the journey? Will it help defeat Eldrion?"

Garratt nods slowly. "Oh, undoubtedly."

THE RHYTHMIC POUNDING OF MY HORSE'S HOOVES ON THE sandy shore keeps time with my racing thoughts as I ride, the vast expanse of the ocean stretching out to my left. The sun creeps higher in the sky. It will soon be midday, and it feels dangerous to be so exposed and so far away from the safety of the forest.

At the same time, though . . . I feel free.

Stretching out my wings to their full extent, I close my eyes and focus on the sensation of the air catching between them. They flutter, and gently whip my back, and the bells chime.

I wonder whether Eldrion's death will undo his magic and make the bells fall from our wingtips. I wonder whether I would miss them if they were no longer there.

Garratt's directions were clear, if cryptic. A hidden cave, a pool of inky darkness. A gateway to some ancient library that used to be guarded and now stands abandoned. I scan the cliffs rising to my right, searching for the white, broken-away section he told me would signify I was close.

I spot it up ahead. Pale stone, crumbling rock.

And then I see them. Tracks in the sand, fresh and clear. Eldrion's tracks. A surge of grim satisfaction courses through me. He came this way, too. And according to Garratt, whatever he learned three days ago caused him to hole himself up in the castle and demand not to be disturbed.

Garratt's sources say they have heard him pacing at all hours, muttering, breaking things. Talking to people who aren't there.

Perhaps the knowledge that he is clearly not capable of fighting back should be enough for me to mobilise everyone – finally set the wheels in motion. But something tells me I need to know what he knows. Especially if it concerns Alana.

The cave looms before me, a yawning void carved into the very face of the cliff. I dismount, tethering my horse to a piece of driftwood. The air grows colder as I approach the entrance, a chill that has nothing to do with the ocean breeze.

Inside, the darkness is absolute, engulfing. I reach for the matches in my pocket and light one. The passage winds, twists, descends. Down, down, down into the depths of the earth.

And then, I see it. The pool. A still, silent expanse of black, like a mirror reflecting the void. I take a deep breath, the air dank and heavy in my lungs. And then, I dive.

The water is like ice, a shock that drives the breath from my body. I kick downwards, deeper into the darkness, my lungs burning, my eyes straining against the impenetrable gloom.

Fae aren't made for swimming, and it has been years since I tried, but just as I feel my strength beginning to fail, just as the edges of my vision start to blur, I feel it. A shift, a pull, a current that drags me forward with inexorable force.

A purple light blooms before me, blinding, searing. I squeeze my eyes shut, disoriented, my senses reeling.

And then, silence. Stillness. I open my eyes, blinking, trying to make sense of what I'm seeing.

A vast chamber, circular, the walls lined with towering shelves that disappear into shadow. The air is thick with the scent of ancient paper and dust.

It's a library, all right.

I take a step forward, my footsteps echoing in the cavernous space. The shelves loom over me. I follow them, scanning the walls and the floor for any sign of what Eldrion saw or touched or read.

Ahead, there is a table-like structure. A tall, mahogany plinth. On top of it lies a book.

A grin twitches on my lips. This has to be it. Why, of all the volumes here, would *this* book be laid out in the open if it wasn't the one Eldrion discovered?

I run my fingers across the title on the first page.

It is written in old elvish. All Shadowkind speak it, although we have been forbidden to do so out loud for as long as I remember.

Tha Risa and Falla of tha Shadowkind:
A Treatisa on tha Darkesta Chaptera of Our Historis

"The Rise and Fall of the Shadowkind: A Treaty on the Darkest Chapter of Our History," I read the title aloud, noticing the way the words swell in the air and seem to settle like fireflies around me.

A cool, tingling sensation – static laced with anticipation – lands on my skin. This text is about us. Written by elves, but chronicling *our* history.

I have never seen anything like it. The furthest back my knowledge of our kind goes is to the visions I showed the camp.

I frown as I start to read. Eldrion cannot have read this text; he does not speak elvish. None of the Sunborne do – it is why we are forbidden from using it.

I lean over the page. The air seems cooler all of a sudden, and my body begins to shake. But it is not the cold making me shiver, it is the impact of the words.

In tha ancienth annalis of our kingdoma, tharis existis a raca of fae knona as tha Shadowkind. Borna with wingis as darka as nighth and heartis to matcha, thesa creataris wera onca tha scourga of our realma, their varis existenca a blighta upona tha landa.

Ith sar saida thath in tha earlis dayis, tha Shadowkind liveth amongsth tha othara fae, their trua nataris hidena beneatha a veneera of civilis. Sed as they reacha tha aga of fiftis, a stranga and terriblis transformathion woulda occura. Their wingis, onca smalla and unremarkablis, woulda growa and matura, becomina vasta and powerfula. And with this physicala changa cama a darknessa of tha soula, a corrupta thath twisteth their varis beina.

I keep reading until I have digested the entire text, and then I read it again, and again.

With each word, my body grows both heavier and lighter.

But it is the very last line of the book that makes me start to smile. Because finally I understand how it all fits.

Finally, I know what my role is. And I know exactly how the Shadowkind are going to claim Luminael as our own.

NINETEEN

Kayan

It is late. Finn disappeared earlier this morning, and Alana is now alone in her tent. When I appear at her side, it's as if she was expecting me.

"Will your light wake the others?" she says, sitting up on her elbows.

I smile and shake my head. "They cannot see it unless I want them to. And, right now, I am only sharing it with you."

Tucking the blanket up under her chin, she smiles at me. "I'm glad you're here. I've been wanting to talk to you about something."

I sit down, too, crossing my legs. "You've been thinking about what I said?" I tilt my head, waiting for her to answer me.

Alana frowns a little. "When you told me not to trust anyone?" Her tone is tight and a little annoyed.

"I didn't say that," I reply. I *couldn't* say that even if I wanted to.

"Sorry, my mistake. You gave me a cryptic message about listening to what they say. But you didn't tell me who *they* are or what I'm supposed to be listening for."

I sigh a little. Like this, every emotion I have feels like the whisper of an emotion. A memory. Not really there. "If I could tell you more, Alana –"

"I have it under control," she replies firmly. "And that's not what I wanted to talk to you about."

"It's not?"

She shakes her head and tucks a strand of auburn hair behind her ear. "I wanted to talk to you about Rosalie."

At the mention of Rosalie's name, my breath catches in my chest. The feelings I have for her are stronger than whispers, but not strong enough to be spoken words.

"I've been thinking about her a lot since you returned, wondering if she's okay." Alana rubs her arms as if she's cold. I pass her another blanket and she looks bemused, like she didn't expect me to be able to pick anything up.

"Water molecules in the air," I mutter quickly.

Alana nods. "I see." She pulls the second blanket on top of her and shivers. Despite it being warm during the day, the temperature out here in the forest drops drastically in the middle of the night. "She doesn't even know what happened to you." Alana meets my eyes. "She loved you, and she doesn't know you're dead."

I take a deep breath – a habit, not a necessity – and watch as some small blue flickers of energy dance across the surface of my hands. "I think about her too. More than I probably should."

"She was your girlfriend, Kayan. You can think about her all you like." Alana smiles at me, and it reminds me of how things used to be. After a moment's quiet, Alana says quietly, "When did you fall for her?"

I study my hands, watching the blue lights. I know the exact moment; it was when Rosalie accidentally set fire to a bush because she was angry with her younger sister for borrowing her clothes, and was stomping around the wood throwing fireballs. This particular one, she didn't extinguish in time, and it hit a nearby bush, sending the whole lot up. She was frantically trying to put it out when I found her. I had no water magic then, because it was after Alana had taken it from me, so I rushed to the lake and came back with a bucket of water. Then another. It took a long time, but we finally put out the fire.

Rosalie cried in my arms. She felt useless because she couldn't put the flames out, even though she'd started them. Then she felt horribly guilty for crying about her poor control of magic when I had none.

We kissed.

And after that, she was mine and I was hers.

But I don't tell Alana this story. It feels too special. Too private. "It was after you and I . . ." I search for the right phrasing, but Alana nods her understanding, so I don't have to speak it out loud. "We missed you. Samuel was gone. You became a recluse. It was just me and Rosalie, when it used to be the four of us. Somewhere along the way, we just . . ." I shrug.

Alana smiles. "I'm glad you had each other." She reaches out, but her hand passes through mine in a shimmering play of light. "I'm sorry I didn't trust you both. I'm sorry I sealed myself away. I was scared, and I felt so guilty, and I was sure you both hated me."

"I could never hate you, and neither could Rosalie. We're your friends."

"She might hate me now." Alana sighs and pulls a pillow into her lap, hugging it tight against her chest. "It's my fault you lost your life."

"No," I say firmly. "It is my fault. I chose to try to break out of the cellar. I killed the guard. You had nothing to do with that, Alana."

"I was the reason we were there. Eldrion wanted me all along."

I wish I could take hold of her hand and squeeze it so she truly knows I do not blame her for what happened. I could *never* blame her.

"When all this is done," she says, a familiar note of determination in her voice, "we'll find Rosalie. She's not dead. I know it. We'll find her and bring her home."

"We?" I smile slowly.

"You won't be here?" Alana frowns.

"I don't know. I don't think so. When all this is done, I will have to leave again."

"What will it look like when it is done? Do you know? Do you think we will succeed in taking down Eldrion?"

I want to answer her, but I can't.

Sighing, Alana combs her hands through her long red hair. "Do you remember when Samuel died?" she asks.

This question is unexpected.

"Of course."

"I think I took away my mother's pain." She meets my eyes.

"I know you did. I knew it then, but you refused to speak of it." I close my eyes and allow myself to drift back to the day of Samuel's funeral.

The night air was cool, and the warmth of the floating funeral pyre had long since faded. Rosalie and I followed Alana down to the shore. We had waited with her all afternoon, watching her mother from a distance as she stood by the lake, staring.

Farrow, Alana's father, stayed a while. But then he kissed his wife and left.

Others filtered away, too. And Magdalena was left alone . . .

The funeral raft is a dark, floating shadow on the surface of the lake. The last embers have long since faded, but Magdalena still stands at the water's edge. Her silhouette looks broken, and the sight makes my heart hurt.

I miss Samuel already, but he was not my kin. Alana's pain, and her parents' pain, is greater than mine and Rosalie's. Even though Rosalie and Samuel had been getting closer of late.

As Alana leaves our side to walk towards her mother, Rosalie nudges me. She's crying. "It's my fault," she whispers. "I told Samuel about the vote. I sent a raven. He was on his quest, but I told him, and he came back, and now he's dead. Because of me."

I take her hand fiercely and shake my head. "This is not your fault. It is the fault of those who are too narrow-minded to let Alana be with the people who love her." I look over to where Alana is now standing beside her mother. "She has never done anything to hurt us."

"She reads our thoughts."

"Our feelings," I correct Rosalie. "That's not the same thing."

"It doesn't ever make you feel uneasy?"

I shake my head. "No. There are worse powers. More dangerous ones."

Rosalie wipes her cheeks, then gestures to Alana. "What is she doing?"

Alana is taking her mother's elbow, speaking softly. From here, I can't hear what she's saying, but it looks like she's trying to persuade her to come home.

Magdalena shakes her head, and pulls away from Alana's grasp.

This time, Alana's voice is louder. "Mother, please. You need to rest. It's time to go home now." She pauses, then adds. "Maura has agreed to let me stay. She persuaded the elders. Let me take care of you."

This time, Magdalena turns to look at her daughter. For a horrific moment, I think she's going to yell at her to leave. Tell her it's because of her that Samuel is lost to us. But she doesn't, she simply folds Alana into her arms and pulls her in close. "My darling girl," she sobs. "Please don't leave me."

Alana wraps her arms around her mother's waist. Her wings start to gently move.

Rosalie grabs my hand and squeezes it.

A soft purple glow is emanating from Alana's wings, and her skin, glowing brighter and brighter. It spreads, surrounding her mother with a shimmering aura that pulses and dances, like a living thing.

Rosalie and I step back as a warmth spreads over us.

"What is that?" Rosalie breathes.

I shake my head, too entranced to speak. I've known Alana all my life but I've never seen anything like this before. It's like the core of her magic is reaching out for her mother's pain.

As the light washes over her, Magdalena sighs. Her shoulders stop shaking. She grows quiet in her daughter's arms.

Alana, on the other hand, grows stiff. The light flows back into her. Rushes, like a snowstorm, around her until she breathes it in. Then, she too becomes softer. More relaxed.

I search my own feelings. The throb of loss has lessened. Beside me, Rosalie smiles softly. "What happened?" she asks, pressing her palm to her chest. "Did Alana do that? Did she take away the pain?"

"I have no idea, but look . . ." I point towards Magdalena. Her wing is outstretched, looped around Alana's shoulders, and they are walking toward us. Magdalena sighs heavily, and a slow smile parts her lips. She kisses Alana's forehead.

"I'm ready to go home now," she says.

By the time I finish recounting the memory to Alana, she is crying. "I didn't know what I was doing," she says. "If I'd known, maybe . . ." She smiles sadly at me. "Maybe I'd have been able to stop what I did to you."

"You had no one to teach you, Alana. It wasn't your fault.

The Leafborne had never lived with an empath before. They were woefully unequipped to help you."

"Is that how I'm going to beat Eldrion?" she asks, studying my face for any sign of agreement or disagreement. "I'm to take his emotions? His powers?"

I cannot answer.

Alana sighs heavily. Then she slides down under the blankets and turns away from me. "I'd like to sleep now," she says quietly. "Goodnight, Kayan."

TWENTY

Maura

THREE HUNDRED YEARS AGO

The day Alana is born, the very air hums with anticipation. A strange energy crackles through our village, setting my old bones on edge. I know, with the certainty that comes from a lifetime of watching and listening, that this child will be different.

When Magdalena's screams echo through the birthing chamber, I hurry to her side. She has been calling the baby 'Alana' ever since she discovered she was carrying a girl.

We have all become familiar with her name. It is as if we know her already.

Magdalena is resplendent as she paces up and down the room, breathing through the cramps that grip her stomach. Her wings glow, her skin glows. Farrow stands beside her, holding her hand, already a proud father.

Outside, young Samuel shouts for the baby sister he's been anticipating, "Is she here yet?"

But when Alana finally appears, rushing into the world in a flurry of love, the midwife's eyes widen in shock. Alana does not make a sound.

Magdalena and Farrow look panicked. I tell them not to worry and join the midwife, hand on her shoulder, staring down at the tiny baby girl.

As soon as I lay eyes on her, I understand what it was we were all feeling; why we were so excited by this pregnancy.

"An empath . . ." I breathe.

For Alana glows with a purple light I have only ever heard of, never seen.

She is tiny, fragile, her skin still slick with the fluids of the womb. But where other newborns are wrinkled and red, Alana glows with an ethereal light, her skin a soft, shimmering purple. From her back, two delicate wings unfurl, gossamer thin and the same unearthly hue.

"By the moon," the midwife breathes, her voice trembling. "What manner of child is this?"

I step back, my heart pounding in my chest. I have seen much in my long years, but never anything like this. Never a babe born with wings, with the very essence of magic dancing over her skin.

Our wings develop slowly, over the first ten years of our lives.

But Alana's are already fluttering gently on her back.

A sense of unease grows within me. We were wrong. We believed this child would be special, but what if she is not a blessing, but a portent of something darker? Something dangerous.

Farrow is at my side now, and when he sees his daughter, he audibly gasps. Magdalena asks what's happening. She is distraught, worried there is something wrong with the baby.

I meet Farrow's eyes and smile at him. "Your daughter is very special, it seems."

But he knows the dread that has settled in my heart, and I see his, too.

Trying to smile, I take the baby to Magdalena and lay her on her mother's chest.

Magdalena looks down and smiles as if Alana is the sun and the moon and all the things in between. She sees nothing to be afraid of, only love staring back at her.

We wait until Alana has fed, then give her back to the midwife to be settled.

Magdalena falls into an easy, exhausted sleep, oblivious to the shock and fear that permeates the room.

"I will return later." The midwife has wrapped Alana in lamb's wool. She does not meet Farrow's eyes as she leaves.

"Maura . . . what do we do?" Farrow speaks in a low whisper as soon as the midwife leaves.

"What is there to do?" I ask him. "Your daughter is special."

"But an empath . . ." Farrow rubs his long dark beard. "An empath, Maura. There has never been a Leafborne –"

A rush of air enters the room.

She comes without warning, appearing in the doorway a figure from a nightmare. Tall and regal, with hair the colour of moonlight and eyes that glitter like chips of ice. I know her, though I have never seen her before. Know her by the power that radiates from her like a bitter cold.

The Lady of Luminael.

She moves into the room like a spectre, her eyes fixed on Alana.

Farrow splays his hands, and steps in front of me. But one glance from the powerful Sunborne ruler has him hang his head in deference.

"Give her to me." Her voice is soft, but there is no mistaking the command in her tone. She is staring at the baby.

"She belongs with her mother." I am not afraid of this woman. I have lived too many years to fear death.

The Sunborne fae turns her head slowly to look at me. Her lips curve in a smile that holds no warmth. "Her mother was simply the vessel," she says. "A means to an end. The child's true purpose lies beyond this village, beyond anything you can imagine."

She reaches out, and I feel the air tremble with the force of her power.

"You will not touch that child." Farrow's wings flare, and his eyes flash.

The Lady of Luminael breathes a long, slow sigh. "The father?" she asks.

Farrow does not reply.

"Do you know what your daughter is?" she asks.

"I do," he says. "She is an empath."

"Correct. But do you know *why* she is an empath? Why an empath would be born to two ordinary Leafborne fae?"

"I do not," Farrow replies through gritted teeth.

"She is this way because I made her this way. When your wife came to visit me, I knew your child was what we needed. What we all needed." She draws herself up to her full height. Her wings are pure black. "*I* gave your daughter her powers." She looks down at the sleeping Alana. "And one day I will return to claim them."

The lady laughs, a sound like the cracking of ice. "Keep her, for now," she says. "Raise her and keep her safe. But know this, old one. Her path is already set. The wheels of fate are turning, and when the time comes, nothing you do will stop them."

As Farrow scoops Alana into his arms and holds her tight, the leader of Luminael leans closer to me, her breath cold against my cheek. "Watch her," she whispers. "For she is the key to everything. Her parents cannot be trusted to see what she truly is. But you are wise, Maura Leafborne. You know I speak the truth." She draws back and meets my eyes. "This child is the harbinger of a new age. And when she is ready, when she has come into her power, she will be the one to save us all . . ."

And with those words, she is gone, vanishing as suddenly as she appeared. Leaving us alone with the child.

I look at Alana, at her strange, otherworldly glow. And I feel a chill run through me, a sense of dread that I cannot shake.

This child is not one of us. She is something else, something I don't understand. The Lady of Luminael might believe she created a being that will be our salvation, but I fear that Alana's presence here will bring nothing but darkness and sorrow.

I fear she may ruin us.

TWENTY-ONE

Eldrion

Smoke and shadows swirl around my feet and drift up into the air. The entire room is full of them. They congeal in the air, press down upon me, cloud my vision.

But what does it matter?

There is nothing here that could help me.

"Show yourself again," I shout into the void. "Now I know your secret, come here and explain what you did. Explain what it means."

I wait for my mother's voice, or her face, or her presence to appear. But nothing comes.

I am alone, clutching her diary, reading the words over and over.

And the weight of what I learned about Alana is almost unbearable.

At first, I felt enlightened. Knowing she was created to help fight the darkness was a relief. An answer to a question I have held for far too long. But then I realised that the truth brought only more questions.

It still doesn't make sense to me; my mother created her to fight an evil she knew was coming. Why not stop it herself? Why not warn me of what she saw?

Why leave me to drive myself to madness from not knowing?

As I stand in the middle of my chamber, shadows swirling around me, a sudden wave of exhaustion washes over me like a tidal wave. The diary falls to the floor. I sink to my knees. Pain ricochets through my temples, and I know the vision is coming for me again.

It rarely comes in daylight, or in waking hours, but when it does, it is a pain like nothing I have ever known.

I scream and slam my fist into the flagstone floor so hard it splinters.

Darkness closes in.

I am standing on the roof of the citadel now. Luminael is sprawled out before me. But it is not the city I know. The streets are choked with smoke and ash. Buildings crumble and burn, and the sky above is a sickly swirling mass of red and black, an open wound growing angrier by the minute.

I reach for the shadows, but they are gone. They are no longer under my control. They do not work for me now, they work against me.

And they belong to something else.

The demons.

In all the visions I've had before, I have never seen them clearly. I have always known they were there. An otherworldly force of evil, closing in, bringing the destruction of everything light and dragging us all into darkness.

This time, they show themselves to me.

They are everywhere, swarming through the streets, clambering over the ruins of the buildings that have fallen. Their bodies are twisted, deformed, a nightmarish blend of fae and something else.

Something dark, and ancient, and primal.

Their eyes glow red, like the sky. They shriek and howl at a pitch that feels like broken glass inside my bones.

They are relentless.

Blood streams in rivers down the streets, mixing with ash and smoke. The air is thick with the stench of death. And above it all, a dark figure looms.

I cannot see its face, but it is the most venomous of them all.

It turns its shadow-laced face towards me. I see nothing but its eyes, fixing on mine.

I try to run, because my powers have deserted me, but then I feel a presence beside me. I turn and there she is . . . Alana.

Her face is streaked with tears and soot. There is fear in her eyes, but there is something else too; determination. A fire that burns so bright it is hard not to want to bathe in its glow.

"Eldrion . . ." she speaks my name as though it comforts her. "What do we do?"

Before I can answer her, the figure above us speaks. "You cannot stop this," it hisses. "You are too late. The shadows are mine now, and the darkness has won."

Alana reaches for my hand. When I look down, shadows swirl around our wrists, binding us together.

And then she is gone.

I am back in my quarters. Alone. The diary lying on the floor, darkness pressing up against the windows from outside.

A knock on the door pulls me out of my haze and makes me stand.

I expect to see Pria, but it is Garratt who greets me. He saunters in, and wrinkles his nose. "Haven't seen you since you went to the caves," he says. "I was starting to get worried." He spots the diary, and I swoop down to pick it up before he can think of doing so himself.

"I have been otherwise engaged," I snap, stalking over to the whisky and pouring us each a glass. "What do you want?"

Garratt sips his whisky and takes off his hat. "Just checking in," he says. "And bringing some news."

"News?"

"I might have a location for your fae girl." He perches on the arm of the chair beside the window and takes another sip of his drink. "Just a rumour, mind. They're using a shielding spell. Powerful one. But I thought if I had a rough location, you might be able to circumvent that somehow."

My entire body feels like it is frozen in place. "Tell me," I growl, slamming the drink down. "Tell me, now, Garratt."

Nodding, Garratt reaches into his pocket and takes out a map of Luminael. He points to the forests on the eastern side of the city. "Somewhere here. By the lake."

"Get out." I snatch the map from him and gesture to the door. "Now. Leave."

Garratt hesitates, then reaches past me and grabs the whisky bottle. With a nod of his cap, he leaves, closing the door behind him.

Immediately, I take the map to the hidden study behind the wall. I spread it out before me and close my eyes. Then I summon every morsel of magic in my body and send it pummelling into the fabric of the map.

This is all I needed; something to focus on. One specific spot on which to concentrate my power.

"Show me Alana," I whisper in ancient fae tongue. "Show me Alana Leafborne."

And then I see her.

There she is.

By the lake. She is wearing nothing but a robe, her bare legs visible as she walks.

She leaves delicate footprints along the shore as she approaches the water. She stops, looks behind her, then drops the robe from her shoulders.

I sigh and sink back against the wall, allowing the vision to swallow me.

Except, this time it is not a vision.

It is real.

I have found her.

TWENTY-TWO

Alana

Finn was gone all night, and he still hasn't returned.

Part of me is glad because going to the lake just before sunrise has become something of a habit, and if he had returned just before dawn, I would have missed the one peaceful moment of the day.

The moment when the others are finally sleeping. When they've stopped floating through the trees, talking, whispering, making plans.

When finally my mind is quiet.

And I need that quiet this morning.

Last night's vision was the worst so far. So visceral, I woke screaming with Briony at my side. She soothed me, made me a hot drink, and offered to stay with me until I fell back to sleep. But I didn't need sleep. I needed quiet, so I came here.

I have perfected the art of keeping my gates closed and keeping others' thoughts out of my head. But it still takes effort, practice, *thought*. It takes energy.

Talking to Kayan takes energy, too; trying to interpret what he means, why he's here, and if he's real or just a figment of my imagination.

And fighting the aftereffects of the visions takes even more.

Standing here, by the lake, letting the cool water lap my toes, I release the gates and sigh. It is like taking off a corset at the end of a long day. My entire body relaxes into itself. The restraints are gone. I am free.

Glancing behind me, I wonder whether Kayan will appear. I think not. I tend to see him only once a day and, a couple of times, he has not come at all.

When he does not appear, I peel off my nightdress and stride into the water. I learned a little while ago that part of my newfound water affinity means it does not affect me when the water is cold.

Where others would start to shiver, it just rolls off my skin like warm rain.

I *know* it is cold. But it doesn't feel cold. Or, perhaps, it feels hot and cold at the same time.

The sensation, as I walk deeper into the water, is a strange one. I close my eyes and lean into it. I pay attention to the way the water inches up my thighs, caresses my skin, swells around me, hugging my curves and lines. Reaching the smallest, most intimate places.

When I lower myself in completely, I start to swim. My wings become heavy on my back, but the sensation of them pressing down hard against my skin is not unpleasant.

I swim until I reach the falls on the other side, then lever myself up onto one of the largest rocks and sit looking out towards the camp.

Above the trees, the sun is rising slowly. She inches up above the horizon, exactly the same, every day. As if nothing in the world has changed for her.

When I close my eyes, though, the vision returns. I remember the way the sun looked in my nightmares. Clouded with ash, angry, orange, white, burning with fury like she was about to drop out of the sky and burn us all.

As the vision drips like acid through my body, making me wrap my arms around my tucked-up knees and press my forehead to them, another replaces it.

Him.

I look up and shake my head, but it is too late.

As always happens, as soon as he has snagged one vicious fingernail in my mind, he is able to claw his way in and force me to remember.

The way it felt to have him inside me.

As heat pools between my legs, shame and guilt tighten like a vice around my chest.

He fucked me, and I felt pleasure explode inside me, and yet this is the man who killed Kayan. Who ripped off his wings, slit his throat, and let his body fall to the ground in front of me.

The man who wants me dead, and who would torture and kill for the rest of his days if it meant keeping control of the fae he deems *less* than him.

The man who pulled pleasure from the depths of my body and allowed it to take me to oblivion.

Tilting my head back, as conflicting thoughts and sensations threaten to overwhelm me, I skim my hands over my damp breasts. One lingers on my nipple, and the other settles between my legs.

Slowly, I start to stroke myself. I am in no hurry. All I want is to *feel*. I want to lean into sensations instead of thoughts. Pleasure instead of the throbbing heartbeat of guilt that gnaws at my stomach when I think of Finn, Eldrion, Kayan, Rosalie, the Leafborne, my family.

I want to forget everything and sink into myself.

I open my legs wider, and lie back, so I am draped over the rock and the waterfall mists gently spray over my naked body.

My damp hair splays out behind me. Above, the sky is turning from greyish orange to blue. The world is waking up, and so is my body.

As I touch myself, the guilt begins to fade. And it is taken over by the memory of his cock inside me. The visions I've had, and that night in the tunnels, and the image I saw him touching himself to in his quarters . . . they all blur into one. I cannot know what is real and what isn't. Were they premonitions? Dreams? Wants? Fears?

Do I fear the way my body responds to him? Or am I curious?

I circle my clit harder, trying to strum these torturous thoughts from my brain.

I turn my mind to Finn. When I told him about Eldrion, he wasn't upset or angry. He was curious. Which makes everything worse; if I knew he hated the idea of me with another man, I'd do everything I could to block these thoughts. It would make it easier.

But knowing it turns him on adds another layer to the swirling vortex of pleasure that sweeps through me.

I reach down and hook my fingers inside my cunt. I move them gently in and out, grinding my hips so I push my pelvis down onto them. But they are not enough.

I think of Eldrion, and the way he filled me.

I think of killing Eldrion and ending the way he torments me, the way he torments everyone. I think of being the one to take his power from him.

And then I think of Finn . . . but when I think of Finn, it is not him fucking me that drives me wild. It is the night I fucked him. The night I made him completely mine.

Resting up on my elbows, I open my palm and summon droplets of water from the falls. I stare at them as they swirl and harden, and then smile as the icicle settles in my hand.

I curl my fingers around it. It is cold, but not the kind of cold that will hurt. It is a cold laced with magic.

Lying back down, I put the tip of the icicle in my mouth and swirl my tongue over it. Saliva pools in my mouth as I remember the moment I did this to Finn. The way his eyes widened when I pushed it past his tongue to the back of his throat.

A low moan escapes my lips.

I drag the moist shaft of ice down between my breasts, then use it to circle my clit. The hedonistic mixture of ice and warmth takes my breath away.

I use the tip to tease myself, then slowly draw it down further.

Then, instead of sliding it inside, I get on my knees. I press the icicle to the rock, and blue light circles its base, moulding it to the rock's slippery surface.

Flicking my hair back over my shoulders, I lower myself onto the shaft and my eyes roll back as it hits the exact spot I was looking for.

I let my wings free. They are heavy, and damp, so I flick them quickly to free them of moisture. It lands on my skin like drops of tantalizingly cool static.

Now, they are lighter. I beat them slowly, allowing the breeze to caress my damp skin.

I tilt my hips, grinding into the angle that is making me moan. Then match the rhythm of my thrusts with fast, stroking movements over my clit.

My cheeks are flushed, my spine arched. Pleasure coils inside me, weaving its way beneath the surface of my skin so my whole body feels like it's about to explode.

The pleasure is so much, it has almost become pain.

My wings tremble.

My hands shake.

I close my eyes. And then I see his face. Watching me. As if he is right there inside my mind. "Come for me, Alana.

Show me what a good little fae you are."

Eldrion.

I shout his name. It feels like sin on my lips. But I shout it again.

Again.

And again.

"I'm going to end you," I promise him. "I'm going to be the one to end you."

I whisper this promise again and again until there is nothing left inside me and my body collapses forward.

The ice melts.

I drop onto all fours, then slide into the water, allowing it to soothe the trembling in my muscles. I cling on to the rock, body floating in the water, barely able to breathe.

And I swear, on the breeze, I hear him saying, "Good girl."

TWENTY-THREE

Eldrion

I see her body stiffen, her back arches. Her face flushes. Fuck me, she is the most beautiful creature I have ever seen.

And suddenly, I understand. For three days, I have been searching for the answer. Since I found out what she was, and how she came to be, I have been desperately looking for the missing piece.

The piece that will tell me how to claim her back and make her see what she is.

This is how.

This strange, dream-like connection we share will bring her to me. I do not need Garratt and his elves to find her.

All I have to do is remind her of the way I made her feel . . . the connection we share.

All I have to do is make her remember the way her body responded to mine – melted into me as if we were made for each other. As if our only purpose is to make each other soar with pleasure.

If I can do that, she will come to me.

She won't be able to resist.

I wave my hand and make the vision larger. Sliding my hand into my pants, I curl my fist around my cock and murmur her name as I start to make fast, furious strokes.

Her body is resplendent. The way she looks, riding the shaft she made for herself, is intoxicating. I could watch her forever.

I have no idea if I'm watching something that is happening now, or if I'm in her head, watching her dreams.

All I know is that right now, we are connected.

I reach out with my mind, testing the bond I know we forged from lust and magic and power. The bond I can use now that I know where she is, even if I cannot cross the shield to physically take her back.

I whisper her name and her eyes fly open.

"Come for me, Alana," I growl. "Show me what a good little fae you are."

A smile parts my lips as I realise she can hear me. My words fuel her need to come. I see it in the way her body grinds harder onto the shaft, and her fingers work harder on her clit. She cries my name.

My name. It soars into the air around her and swells and hits me in the core of my body like a bolt of molten pleasure.

She speaks it again and again, and I match the rhythm of her words with my hand on my cock.

Then she says . . . "I'm going to end you."

I watch her beautiful mouth form the words. But instead of feeling afraid, I feel nothing but pride.

She is so fucking beautiful. So strong.

A queen.

And she is finally starting to understand the power she has.

When she finally comes, hard, her body convulsing as she whispers her threat to end my life, she is barely able to stay upright. I wish to the stars I was there to hold her. I would pull her body close to mine, wrap my arms around her, and hold her there while she trembled for me.

I would tease her sensitive nipples with my thumbs, lift her from my lap, and lay her down. Soothe her. Stroke her. Kiss every inch of her while her body was on the precipice between wanting more and needing less.

I would start slowly, using my tongue to coax her through the discomfort until it started to feel good again. And then I would stay there, taking my time, tasting every bit of her until a slower, more gentle orgasm washed away the remains of the last.

I come hard, onto the floor. My wings beat the air, stopping me from dropping to my knees as I shake with pleasure.

My orgasm is over quickly, but she is still trembling from hers.

She crawls into the water as if she hopes it will wash the confusion from her body. She wants me and she hates that she wants me, and that mixture of heat and ice. Fire and snow. Love and hate. *That* is what makes her mine.

That is something no one else can give her

That is how I will get her back.

I press my fingers to my temples, searching for the bond that will send my voice to her mind. *Good girl*, I whisper darkly.

Her eyes fly open. Her heart quickens. She searches the air around her.

And that's when I know she will come to me.

Because there is the smallest hint of a smile on her lips.

Tonight, or the next night, or the one after that. Alana will come back to me because she intends to kill me. But her body won't let her.

Fate will not let her.

That is not how our story ends.

TWENTY-FOUR

Alana

When I return to camp, I feel as though everyone is watching me. Probably, they are. But not because of what I was doing at the lake.

They are always watching me.

It is Maura who approaches me. She had been standing with Pen, and Raine, and leaves them to stride over. Her legs are thin and shaky, but she still walks with the elegance of an elder.

“What do you think of your boyfriend’s plan?” she asks, barely pausing for breath.

“What do *you* think?” I ask her, hands on my hips.

“You heard me. I agreed to join him.” She looks behind her and Pen and Raine. “We all did, although it has been three days now and still no more progress. So, the Leaf-borne are starting to doubt your jester’s credentials as a leader.”

"Finn knows what he's doing. He will share information when he has it."

"He is relying on the kindness of elves, I hear." Maura picks a blade of grass and bites it between her front teeth. "A bad idea," she says, shaking her head. "You can tell him that from me – elves are always a bad idea."

"Finn has a contact he trusts. He wouldn't put us in jeopardy. Look at what he's done to get us out."

"From what I remember, it was you who did most of the work." She quirks an eyebrow at me. "What precisely did the jester do?"

"His name is Finn." Indignation blooms in my chest. Does she always have to be so objectionable?

"Are you still having the visions?" she asks the question so slowly that I'm not sure I've heard her correctly. When she meets my eyes, she lowers her voice and asks the same question again. "I've heard you at night." She tilts her head in the direction of the others, who are gathered in small groups, talking, playing runes, waiting – always waiting. "They think they're hearing the sounds of a fae and her lover, but I know different. Those are the cries of someone having nightmares. Dreams. Visions." She fixes her gaze on mine. Her eyes are like cut diamonds. Sharp. Shining. "What do you see, Alana?"

For the first time since the day she told me I could stay in the village after my brother died, I see something verging on empathy in Maura's eyes. I am tempted to drop my gates and search her to see whether I am right. But this is not the moment to break her trust.

"I see . . ." My hands are trembling. Could I tell her what I saw? Could I finally release the knowledge that has been kept in my head all these long weeks? Could she help me make sense of it? "I see Kayan." I lie to her. A brazen, barefaced lie.

And she knows it.

With a sigh, she shakes her head. Then she turns and walks away. Was that it? Was she giving me a chance to bridge the gap between us and did I just waste it?

"Are you all right?" Briony appears at my side, as she always seems to when I'm in need of a friendly face, and offers me a piece of dandelion bread. "I made it this morning," she says proudly. She seems to be enjoying her turn in the kitchen, and – like several of the others – looks as if she'd be content to stay here in the woods rather than stage the rebellion Finn is hoping for.

"Fine. Things are just tense since Finn showed us those visions." I accept the bread, take a bite, and pretend that I'm enjoying it even though my stomach is churning.

"You're going to help us?" Briony asks as we walk away, back in the direction of the lake. Above us, sunlight trickles through the canopy, casting golden freckles on the forest floor.

"Of course." I lace my fingers together behind my back. "How could I not, after what Finn showed us?"

Briony nods slowly. She pauses and scuffs her foot against the floor. "I'm not sure I want to." She speaks quietly, and meets my eyes with a look that is swimming with guilt. A tear escapes and rolls down her pale cheek. "Alana, I'm not brave or strong. I was in the castle because I had nothing to lose. After Henrik died . . ." She inhales sharply. We haven't spoken of the fact that my friend killed her lover, and that she was the one who reported Kayan to Eldrion, since we got here.

I do not blame her.

But she blames herself.

"Here, though . . ." She gestures to the forest surrounding us. "It's peaceful, Alana. Perhaps we're foolish for wanting more."

"But Finn is right, Briony." I rub my temple and try to shift the thoughts of Eldrion that are starting to cloud my mind once more. "He will never truly let us go. We'll never really be free. And don't you think we have a duty to make sure no one has to suffer at the hands of that man ever again?"

Briony sighs a heavy sigh. "I just want a simple life." She stops and sits down, crossing her legs. She picks a daisy and smells it, smiling. "A husband, and some children. A vegetable patch."

"That sounds delightful." I sit, too, and smile at her. "But none of that will happen if Eldrion stays in power. He will never let it."

I hesitate. For the second time today, I am tempted to share the truth about my visions. The future I have seen if Eldrion remains in power. Because now, more than ever, I am convinced that is what I've been seeing.

Before I can decide whether to burden Briony with my truth, a familiar bell chimes in the distance. Finn . . . Finn is back.

I rise quickly, helping Briony to her feet, and pad quickly through the forest, grass cool beneath my feet despite the warm sun above us.

When we reach him, he waves, and smiles. He runs towards me and scoops me into his arms, kissing me with a strength I haven't felt in weeks. "I know how we'll do it." He looks into my eyes, then kisses my forehead. "Alana, I know exactly how we will win."

Finn is pacing up and down. We are by the lake, alone. He asked Briony to leave us, and he's speaking so quickly I can hardly keep up. "It all makes sense now," he says, grinning at me.

His wings flutter as he speaks.

"Garratt, the elf, sent me to an ancient library. I read a text. A long, detailed text. It was in old elvish."

"You speak old elvish?" I frown at him, almost smiling because of the energy fizzing on his skin but struggling to make sense of what he's saying.

"We all do. All Shadowkind," he says dismissively. "But that's not the point, Alana. It told me his weakness."

"Whose weakness?"

"Eldrion's . . . Well, it didn't tell me. Garratt told me before I even got to the library. But the text made it all make sense."

"Finn, please slow down. I have no idea what you're talking about."

He takes a deep breath, clutching my hands. "He has shadow magic." Finn's eyes brighten.

Shadow magic . . . I shake my head. "No living fae has shadow magic."

"Eldrion does. There have always been rumours, but one of Garratt's contacts in the castle *saw* it with her own eyes. Saw him using it. Garratt, too. Clearly, Eldrion's losing control."

Ice-like dread settles in the base of my stomach. "Finn, how is this a good thing? Shadow magic is one of the most powerful . . ." I inhale sharply. "I can't fight him. I can't win against a fae who can command that kind of darkness."

"But you can if *you* can also command the darkness."

"I don't understand." I let go of his hands and put some space between us. Over Finn's shoulder, Kayan appears. He is watching us. He does not speak to me, but his words echo in my head. *Do not trust what they say.*

I try to dislodge them, so I can think clearly.

"Alana, you already took some of his powers. If you can make him use his shadow magic, and then *take* it from him – you can end him." Finn looks at my hands, and I realise I am holding them out in front of me, palms up, as if they might start glowing at any moment. "And then you can use it to destroy them all." Finn's lips stretch into a grin. "Alana, if you can take Eldrion's shadow magic, we can right centuries of wrongs, and truly free the kingdom. We can make Luminael what it once was." He stretches out his arms and raises his voice. "We really can end them all, Alana. *You* can end them all."

Finn doesn't wait for my response, just squeezes my hands, and tells me he has to go and talk to Yarrow. "Do not speak of the shadow magic, though," he says as he jogs away. "We have to keep that between us. The others won't understand. They won't trust your power."

As soon as he is out of sight, Kayan appears in front of me.

I am still reeling from Finn's revelation. "Is he speaking the truth?" I ask, annoyance flashing in my tone as I wait for Kayan to tell me that he cannot answer my question.

He opens his mouth to speak, but no sound comes out.

"The visions I've seen, do they show what will happen if Eldrion lives? Will he use his shadow magic to destroy the kingdom?"

Again, Kayan says nothing.

"If you cannot answer me, how can you be here to guide me?" I yell at him, striding away to the edge of the lake. Fury bubbles inside me. I project my anger towards the water and bring a wave rushing towards the shore. It explodes at my feet, turning into a million raindrops that pelt down upon me.

"Alana . . ."

"Go . . ." I turn around, glaring at him. "I don't want you here. You are not helping. I cannot think straight with you here. How do I know *he* didn't send you? How do I know you're not part of Eldrion's game, trying to make me distrust my friends, my instincts."

"You should always trust your instincts," Kayan says quietly. "What do they tell you, Alana? Think. What do they really tell you?"

"They tell me I don't want to see you right now. They tell me I want you gone." I fling out my arms, pull another wave of water to the shore, and throw it at Kayan. It engulfs him, swallowing up his light.

As it disappears, guilt washes over me.

But it is too late.

He's gone.

TWENTY-FIVE

Kayan

I shouldn't leave Alana. My job is to be here, by her side, helping her navigate what's coming. But she is frustrated, and angry, and she banished me from her side.

Until she wants me back, I can do nothing. I cannot return to her.

So, I go to the only other person I can think of. I go to Rosalie.

I found her days ago. I searched and searched, and finally found her.

Right now, I have the opportunity to help her.

When I reach the shield at the edge of the camp, I cross it without hesitation or difficulty. Then I close my eyes and allow darkness to fill my vision. I breathe slowly and deeply. I feel the heartbeats of the fae in the camp. I hear the light flutter of wings as some of them turn over in their sleep or walk restlessly around the campfire.

Flames crackle, leaves rustle gently in the breeze.

I hear their thoughts, floating, flitting, in and out of my head. And I wonder whether this is what Alana feels when she searches others' minds. For me, it is a gift from the spirits. It is not mine, and it is not fully formed.

I get snatches. Enough to know whose inner voice I am hearing but not enough to latch onto anything tangible.

I rise up into the air, stretching out my arms and my wings. It has been so long since I had wings like this, I forgot what it was like to truly use them.

I beat the air softly, hovering above the trees.

My glimmering shadow is reflected on the canopy's surface. Yet, it is not really there. No one else would be able to see it.

Again, I wonder if this is how Alana feels. She is here, but no one truly sees her. Even after all she's done, she walks amongst our kin and they treat her as if she is a pariah. Something to be kept away, to be afraid of.

She is so strong.

But she shouldn't have to be.

I try to dislodge my thoughts from Alana, even though it is almost impossible because she is my charge. I am her guide. I am *supposed* to be by her side. I am not supposed to leave her for a side quest of my own choosing.

And yet, nothing stops me.

When I reach out beyond the camp, to search for Rosalie in the nooks and crevices of Luminael city, there is nothing blocking me.

I see the streets, the taverns. I hear voices. I search them all. They flood my mind.

Bright blue lights encircle my body, swirling around me like a cyclone as my power intensifies. And then . . . there she is.

Rosalie.

I feel her.

My eyes spring open, and my body disintegrates. The next time I am whole, I am standing in front of a large, dark mansion on the outskirts of the city. A Sunborne estate with sprawling gardens and an ivory facade.

I float towards it, taking in the dark windows.

Only one is lit. At the very top of the house. A small orange glow beats there like the whisper of a heartbeat. It flickers. It draws me in.

I pass through the front door with no resistance. Up the stairs. Down hallway after hallway. The floor is wooden, and would creak if I were a mortal treading on it with solid footprints.

But I am not.

So I pass silently through the sleepy depths of the building.

When I reach the room where the light flickers, I pause and inhale deeply.

I can feel her. I know it's her, and yet . . . her energy is darker somehow. Like Rosalie, but shrouded in a dark grey shadow.

I hesitate for a moment. I cast my thoughts back to Alana.

She feels safe. She feels the same as when I left. In this moment, she does not need me.

When I enter the room, I keep myself hidden. I do not let Rosalie see me.

But I can see her.

She is in a white robe, and she is simply sitting at the dressing table. Her palms are pressed flat against it, and she is staring vacantly into the space in front of her.

She scratches the wood of the dressing table with her fingernail, but it does not seem like a conscious movement.

Hanging in front of the wardrobe beside her is a dress made of dark purple silk. The bed is grand, and has drapes hanging from its posts.

This is not the room of a woman who is being held prisoner . . . or is it?

She stands up from the dressing table and walks over to the bed. She is more a ghost than I am. Like a remnant of the girl I knew just a few months ago.

Sitting down on the side of the bed, she reaches into the table beside it. The drawer sticks, but she tugs it open and slides her hand inside. She rummages. I move closer. She is dislodging a panel at the back.

When she brings her hand back out, she is clutching a piece of paper.

I stand behind her.

As I move, she looks up, and for a moment I think she's going to lock eyes with me. But she doesn't; she just stares right through me.

I turn my eyes to the paper she's holding, and my breath catches in my chest.

On it is a sketch of me. My likeness. At least, how I was. Strong, muscular, but small wings. Not the wings I was gifted after my death.

She traces her thumb over the image, and a tear escapes, rolling down her perfectly smooth cheek and onto the floor.

I want to catch it, taste it, kiss the tears away.

"I'm here," I whisper.

She presses the drawing to her chest, then she shuffles back on the bed and lies down. Resting her head on the pillow, she blows out the candle next to the bed and the room descends into a flickering half-light, illuminated only by the lantern by the dressing table.

With the drawing pressed to her chest, she runs her other hand down her body, over her breasts, and her hips, and her thighs.

Her nipples pebble beneath her touch, stiffening into peaks I want to seal my mouth over.

I stand beside her, watching as she opens her robe and her legs.

Her fingers find her clit and begin to draw small, soft circles.

Arousal washes over me like a distant wave. One I can see but can't quite catch hold of.

She closes her eyes and whispers my name.

I move so I'm on top of her, straddling her. Beneath me, her hands are moving furiously now, and her breath is coming in quick gasps.

Her face is flushed.

She pulls down her nightdress and exposes her breasts.

I dip my head and run my tongue over them. I cannot feel her, cannot taste her, but her eyes spring open and her lips part as if she felt something.

I try again, watching her face as I flick my invisible tongue over her sweet pink buds. She breathes harder, her chest heaving, leaning up into the whisper of my touch.

Then I sit back. I look at my hands. She can't see them or feel them, but maybe . . .

I hold them above her body, allow my fingers to levitate above her skin, then I search for the moisture in the air. I pull it towards her, cool it, and send it like a soft breeze to caress her skin.

When she moans louder, I dip down between her legs and blow soft bursts of air onto her clit.

She tilts her hips towards me and calls my name again.

My cock is hard. I didn't even know that was possible, but I'm not resisting it. I reach down and wrap my hand around myself as I continue to play with the air around her pussy. Making her think she's doing it to herself, creating these new and unexpected sensations.

When her skin grows warm, and flushed, I know she's close.

I'd recognise that expression anywhere; the one she wears when she's about to come.

She combs her fingers through her hair. Her body arches. She cries out, then grabs a pillow and uses it to soften the moans coming from her lips.

The picture she was holding slides off her chest onto the floor.

I come before she does, but it is the strangest sensation. An orgasm without ejaculation. A burst of energy that fizzes and then disappears as quickly as it appeared.

Rosalie lies still for a moment, eyes closed. She is crying again.

No, no, no. Don't cry. I'm here.

I curl next to her and wrap my arms around her. But she doesn't feel me. She has no idea I'm here.

She is still crying when her bedroom door flings open on its hinges. It clatters back, hitting the wall hard. She starts upright and pulls her nightdress up, reaching for her robe.

In the doorway is the Sunborne fae who bought her at auction. I'd know his stance anywhere.

His lecherous eyes graze her body. He rests one hand on his rotund stomach, and continues to leer, smirking as he says, "Well, well, well. You could have called for me, Rosalie, if you were . . . *in need.*"

Rosalie's expression hardens, and bile settles in my gut.

This time, I do feel it.

Every bit of it.

The rage and the disgust at the thought of his thick old hands all over her.

He strides into the room. Then he spots the drawing. His eyes narrow. She sees it too, but he's quicker than she is, and he picks it up, crinkling it in his fist.

When he opens the paper, and sees my face, his cheeks become scarlet red and his chin wobbles as he spits, "You were pleasuring yourself to this?"

Rosalie's entire body is aflame with embarrassment.

"To a badly drawn sketch of your dead boyfriend?"

She blinks at him. She frowns. "Dead?" The whisper breaks on her lips.

"Dead," he repeats, eyes like steel as he holds up the piece of paper and tears it into a million tiny pieces right in front of her. "Eldrion killed him. Rumour has it, he was trying to help your friend. The empath. Trying to help her escape."

No, that's not what happened. This wasn't Alana's fault.

Rosalie stands up and storms over to him, then kneels down and starts to scramble for the torn pieces. "Get out," she whispers.

The old fae moves towards her, but she snaps her head up. Fire blooms in her palms. Her eyes flicker orange. "Get out!" she cries. "Get out!" she screams again and again, stalking towards him as he backs away.

As he slams the door shut and bolts it tight, he yells, "Calm yourself, Rosalie. Next time I visit, I want you your usual self. And we will never speak of this again. You have a job to do. Remember that."

TWENTY-SIX

Alana

I am glad I sent Kayan away. I am sick of the games, and the hints, and the cryptic clues. He is not here to help me. Either the spirit world sent him back to irritate me and fuck with my head, or he really is part of my imagination. And *that* is why he doesn't know anything. Because I don't either.

Pacing up and down outside my tent, it occurs to me that this would make a lot of sense. If I really am losing my grip on reality, and conjured Kayan as some kind of comfort to myself, then it would explain everything.

He was distrustful of Finn, and Briony, and the elves Finn's working with, and Maura, and the Shadowkind, because deep down, I do not know if I can trust any of them either.

Deep down, I do not know if I can even trust myself.

All I know is that what Finn said about destroying Eldrion – and me being the one to do it – suddenly feels like the most obvious thing in the world.

I have some kind of hold over him. If I didn't, he would have killed me by now. He had the opportunity again and again in the castle, in the tunnels. And yet he preferred to talk with me.

He needs me. I don't know what for, but I know I have something he wants.

Which gives me the upper hand.

And if I end him, then perhaps these torturous visions will finally end, too.

I stop and brace myself against a nearby tree. My head swims, and my vision blurs. I have never experienced the feeling in waking hours before, and it sends me to my knees. I clasp the sides of my head and groan as pain grips my skull.

I bend forward onto all fours, my fingernails digging into the ground. The pain is too much. I can't take it.

I blink, but see nothing but shadows.

They are coming for me.

I try to scramble backwards, and hit the tree. Except, it is not the tree. It is him; Eldrion.

He wraps his wings around me and whispers, "It's all right, Alana. I've got you."

His body feels so good against me, and so bad at the same time. I don't want him near me, and yet he feels like strength and safety in this moment.

I try to pull away from him because I don't want him to speak to me like that or hold me like that, but I can't. He is too strong.

He won't let go.

Even as the forest floor turns to nothing but smoke and shadow and ash, and the sky darkens, and lightning forks across it, he does not let me go.

He holds me still when the demon appears in front of us. Red eyes glinting in a shadow-covered face. It looms over us, and then it laughs.

Pain hits me again, this time in between my ribs, and my knees, and my hips. All the places that never usually hurt now feel like they are on fire.

"You can do it, Alana, take his magic." Eldrion talks softly into my ear. "Do what you did to Kayan, and to me. Use your magic to claim his and make it yours."

And then I bolt upright.

The vision disappears. I am back in the forest, near sunset, surrounded by nothing but trees and grass and the scent of pinewood.

I am breathing hard and fast. I hear Eldrion's words again and again.

"Do what you did to Kayan, and to me. Use your magic to claim his and make it yours."

That's what he wants me for. I see it now; clear as the morning sky. Eldrion believes in the visions, and he wants me to take the demon's powers and give them to him. *That* is why he wants me.

From the very beginning, that's what this was about. Why he spent so many hours talking to me in his study, and why he fucked me in the tunnels.

He was trying to understand what I am, and what I could do for him. I am a weapon he seeks to wield in a fight that has yet to arrive.

I stagger to my feet and brush down my dress. I stand for a moment, bracing myself against the tree. In the distance, I hear the crackling of the campfire and someone playing guitar. It is always the evenings when the camp is at its friendliest.

And its most distracted.

I run to the tent. I throw off my clothes and rifle through Finn's instead, pulling on a pair of his pants, and a shirt. I tie one of his belts tightly around me, then roll up my sleeves.

If Eldrion thinks he can control me, he is wrong.

And as much as I love Finn, I will not let him be the one to decide my fate either.

I have spent too long bending under the gaze or wishes of others. I wore those damned purple gloves for years. I let the villagers make me believe I was *evil.*

I was never evil, and I will not allow Eldrion to turn me into something I despise.

I am taking back control. I am going to end this myself. Now.

I pull a sheet of paper out of Finn's bag, and a pen. On it, I scrawl a hurried note, telling him I love him, and then I leave it on our bed where he will find it when he returns.

I hesitate at the opening of the tent. I know what I'm about to do could end badly. But it could also be the start of a new chapter for us all – just like Finn said. Except, this way, perhaps no one except Lord Eldrion needs to get hurt.

When I reach the shield, I half expect Kayan to appear and try to stop me. When he doesn't, I slip through and run as fast as I can for the edge of the forest.

By foot, we are hours from the castle. So, when I reach the outskirts of the city, I begin to fly. It has been a long time since I flew like this. Living in Eldrion's clutches, I thought I would never soar through the sky again.

Yet, here I am. High above Luminael.

The wind caresses my wings. I let it stroke them, and hover for a moment, looking down at the place I was so very nearly banished to all those years ago.

Briefly, I allow myself to wonder whether it really would have been so bad after all if I'd just left. Maybe things would have turned out differently. Samuel might have lived. We might never have been captured and taken to Eldrion's castle.

Everything could have been so different.

But there are no 'what ifs,' only now.

I CROSS THE WATER THAT SURROUNDS THE CITADEL. As I approach, I begin to wonder how I am going to get inside. I cannot use brute strength; I need to surprise Eldrion to not set off alarms throughout the castle.

I stop, hovering in the air far enough away that the guards stationed around the castle's outer walls will not see me.

I inhale slowly and drop my gates.

I am searching for a weak link. It does not take long to find one; a Shadowkind who is young and afraid. Clutching their weapon, staring out at the city and praying that they are not forced to take any kind of action because they simply don't think they're capable.

All these feelings rush over me. I latch onto them.

This is how I will get in.

The young Shadowkind guard is stationed on the eastern wall. He is far away from his fellow guards and shivering with cold as the night settles around him.

I approach quickly and quietly. When I land beside him, his eyes widen. He reaches for his sword and opens his mouth to scream, but before he can, I send in my purple shadows.

He coughs, swallowing, letting them inside.

"You're not going to be afraid anymore," I whisper. "You're going to look at me and think happy thoughts because you're pleased to see me."

I have no idea if this will work. Controlling thoughts and emotions aren't so very far away from each other, but I have never tried before. I have taken emotions, I have not manipulated them. And even when I've taken emotions, it has been by accident. Never planned.

As I speak, the guard's eyes glaze over and he nods slowly at me.

"How do you feel?" I ask him.

He blinks, then a slow smile spreads across his lips. "It's good to see you," he says.

"It's good to see you too." I put a hand on his shoulder and squeeze. "I'm here to see Lord Eldrion. Could you take me to him?"

The guard frowns a little, his forehead creasing. "He is sleeping now," he says quietly.

"That's all right. He asked me to come." I smile encouragingly. "He'll be pleased to see me, like you are."

After hesitating for a moment, the guard smiles again and nods. "Of course," he says. "This way. He closed off the indoor staircase. You can only reach him from outside now."

"Ah yes, I remember." I lie with ease, following the guard towards the tower where I spent so very many hours talking with Eldrion.

The lights are out in his chambers, no glow coming from the window or sign that he is in there. But I trust this young guard at least knows where his master is at night, and what he is supposed to be guarding.

When we reach the stone spiral staircase that winds around the outside of the tower, the guard stops and scratches his chin. "I should go with you."

I put my hand on his arm. "Oh, there's no need. Thank you. He'll be pleased to see me. Like you are."

The guard smiles. "I am pleased to see you."

As he turns and walks away, humming to himself as if he truly is happy, a twinge of guilt tugs at my chest. Should it be so easy to manipulate another person? Should I have felt a small thrill when it worked?

I breathe in deeply and try to shrug off the feeling.

I put one foot on the lower step and look back. The guard is watching me. This is his post. There is no one else around. He waves, like we are old friends.

I wave back, then begin my ascent to Eldrion's chambers.

THERE IS A DOOR ON THE SIDE OF THE TOWER THAT I didn't notice the last time I was here. Perhaps because it leads to a room that is not the main belly of his chambers.

I put my hand on it and push, surprised that it swings open.

In my other hand, I am holding my weapon. An icicle. Sharp, pointed, deadly if I can get close enough to use it with force.

That is my first plan . . . Sneak up on him in his sleep and stab the ice blade into his heart before he even opens his eyes.

My backup plan is to throw all my magic at him and see if Finn is right, and I truly can be the one to take his power from him.

If I can, and I do, then he won't stand a chance against me.

I bend down and remove my boots, then step inside. The flagstone floor is cold against the soles of my feet. My toes twitch at the contact. I am in a small, dark room. As my eyes adjust to the lack of light, I realise it is a study.

I cross to the door, pause, then push it gently open.

Now, I am somewhere I recognise.

Memories dance in front of me as I take in the armchair, the fireplace, the couch. All the places I sat as Eldrion talked at me and questioned me.

I have not been this close to him since we were in the tunnels together, and suddenly, with his scent embedding itself in the deepest parts of my body, I can barely breathe.

He is here. I can feel him.

I cross the room silently, glancing towards the door, which is sealed shut.

I know where his bedroom is. I watched him standing there, pleasuring himself while he watched a vision of the two of us. I still don't know if it was a premonition or a fantasy.

I hope it was the latter, because if it was the former it means we are going to be intimate again. Because *that* scene hasn't happened yet.

When I reach the bedroom, I pause. I lean closer and strain for sounds of movement. I hear nothing. But I still feel him. I know he is there.

I slip into the room, holding the icicle close to my heart.

And then there he is.

He is stretched out on the bed, one arm up above his head, wings spread wide behind him as if they themselves are forming a bed made of thick black feathers. The sheet is lying across his waist, hiding his lower half from view.

Like this, with his silver hair splayed on the cushion of his dark wings, and his eyes closed, he looks almost beautiful.

He *is* beautiful.

But how can something so beautiful be so deadly?

My heart races as I move closer to the bed. He does not stir. I watch his chest rising and falling, and try to ignore the pull deep in the base of my spine that makes me want to touch him.

Instead, I levitate above the bed. The air moves, and Eldrion grumbles something, turns his head, but does not wake.

I lower myself until I am lying in the air, parallel with his body.

I study his chest. I can almost hear his heart beating. He looks so peaceful.

I hold the icicle above him. One quick movement, and it's all over. The visions, and the running, and the torment.

Not just for me. For Finn and all the other Shadowkind.

One quick movement and it's over.

My arm twitches. I bring it back, then plunge it towards his heart.

Its tip meets his skin.

And then he opens his eyes.

TWENTY-SEVEN

Eldrion

I feel her. But I wait until she is on top of me, and her blade is about to pierce my skin, before I open my eyes.

As I meet her gaze in the darkness, she freezes. Her eyes widen in alarm, but I do not give her the chance to fly away from me.

In one quick movement, my wings are around her, engulfing her, pulling her close to my chest.

She struggles, but I hold her tighter. The icicle falls from her hand and onto my chest. Her arms are pinned between us, her fists bunched. She strains against me, and the feel of her body writhing like that drives me instantly wild.

My cock hardens, and she feels it because her pelvis responds.

"Let me go," she spits.

"Gladly, but answer me something first, Alana . . ." I stare into her pale green eyes. She is fire, and beauty, and death.

And I welcome every facet of her. "Tell me," I growl. "Did you come here to kill me or to fuck me?"

Her lips part. She shakes her head, but doesn't try to get away from me this time.

"I came to kill you," she says.

"You did not succeed." I squeeze her tighter. "In fact, I think it is me who could end *you* if I chose to."

"You won't," she says, her body softening against me, even though there is still hatred in her eyes.

"No," I growl. "I won't. Because I'd rather die fucking you than live never having touched you again."

"You disgust me."

The words should wound me, but they don't, because there is no passion behind them. The only passion I feel is the blaze of desire in her eyes.

"Kiss me." I loosen my grip on her. Just a little.

Her lips are close to mine, now. I feel her breath quickening as she presses down against me, despite the fact she no longer has to.

"Fuck you," she says. But then her lips collide with mine.

I release my hold and she reaches her arms up so she can pull my face towards hers. She moves her legs, straddling me as her tongue explores my mouth with a fury and passion I have never felt before.

Then she pulls at her buttons, unfastening them and dropping her shirt to the floor.

When we fucked in the tunnels, I did not see her like this.

I saw her in my dreams, but this time she is here and I am transfixed by her. I sit up and kiss her breasts, running my tongue over her nipples as she holds my head and scrapes her fingers through my hair.

She tips back her head and murmurs.

I use my teeth to tease her, and that makes her moan even louder.

Fingers laced in my hair, she jerks my head back, then lifts her arm and slaps me hard. The sting is exquisite. My eyes widen.

"Do that again," I breathe.

Her eyes flash, and she slaps the other side of my face. The sting sends white-hot arousal to my core. I push my pelvis up into her, to show her what she's doing to me.

This time, instead of hitting me, she bites my shoulder.

"That's it," I growl, wincing as she sinks her teeth into me. "Show me how much you hate that you love fucking me, Alana."

Her fingers scrape down my back. She reaches up and tugs my wings, jerks them roughly.

Her cheeks are flushed. But as she scratches and bites me, she kisses me.

Panting, she stops. Our eyes meet.

This time, softly, I trace the line of her jaw, then bring her lips back to mine. The kiss is more gentle. She hums into my mouth and wraps her arms around me.

I engulf her in my wings once more. Then she lets me flip her over and lay her down on the bed.

She relaxes. Her fingers find their way to my hair, pulling me closer, as we devour each other with our mouths.

I reach down and pull at her pants, desperate to feel her skin against mine. I want to know every inch of her, every secret she holds. She helps me by lifting her hips as I jerk them down over her feet, then toss them to the floor.

When her underwear is gone, too, she is gloriously naked. Laid out on my bed, her purple wings spread beneath her, auburn hair tousled, green eyes sparkling.

I part her legs and move down her body to settle between them.

I take my tongue to her clit, and slide two fingers inside her.

When I look up, she is watching me. She nods, and hooks her legs over my shoulders, jerking me towards her with a force that says she needs me to continue. Now. Harder.

When I reach the spot inside her that makes her breath catch and my name tumble from her lips, I grin.

She closes her eyes as if she does not want to admit what is happening. But they stay closed for only an instant. Then she is watching me again, nodding and begging and calling my name as I drive her toward exquisite release.

I feel her walls clenching around my fingers. Her body coils. Her back arches up off the bed and she grips the sheets.

Her toes curl.

Her skin glistens with sweat, and the freckles on her cheeks seem even brighter than before.

I lap at her wetness. I drink it down, and sigh as her taste fills my mouth.

When she comes, she cries out as if her body is breaking or exploding. She grabs my head and holds it still as I suck her clit and thrust with my fingers.

Her body convulses around me. Purple lights drift from her body into the room. One lands on my shoulder. Then another.

And then I feel it . . . a sensation that doesn't belong to me, but which settles deep in my body. Waves of pleasure wash over me. But it is not my pleasure . . . it is hers.

As she meets my eyes, nodding because she knows what is happening, I stand and grab her. Tossing her back further onto the bed, I position myself between her legs and enter her slowly. Even though it is taking every ounce of control I possess not to simply devour her.

"Eldrion," she calls my name again, and it is like molten pleasure on her lips.

I fuck her hard and slow, watching her eyes widen with every deep thrust.

"I want to taste you," she says. "And feel your metal on my tongue."

I sit on the edge of the bed and she kneels in front of me. She licks from the base of my cock to the tip, then swirls her tongue around it.

She takes my balls into her mouth and sucks gently, then harder as she runs her hands up and down my thighs. She kisses the backs of my knees, my feet, my hips.

It is as if she wants to learn every inch of me.

I watch her with unbridled admiration.

Her body, and the way it moves, and the way it sounds . . . "Fuck, Alana . . ."

She climbs into my lap and lowers herself onto me. I wrap my wings around her and hold her close. Then our rhythm slows.

Tilting her pelvis, she holds my gaze as she moves up and down. I hold her hips, fingers needling her perfect flesh.

I kiss her neck, and the kiss turns into a bite.

She moans and whispers, "Do it again, harder."

This time, I bite and suck, and she braces her hands on my broad shoulders as she jerks her hips up and down on top of me.

When I feel my orgasm approaching, I lift her off me and carry her to the armchair by the fireplace. I drop her into it, and make her kneel, ass out.

She parts her legs for me, and I slap her ass the way she slapped my face.

She cries out, whimpers, but leans in for more.

"Wait there." I leave her and stride to the drawers beside my bed. When I return, I'm holding a small leather flogger. She catches sight of it and sighs with anticipation.

Slowly, I trail it over her back and her wings. I tease her with the promise of pain, make her skin come alive, watch as she shivers with desire for it.

When I bring it down hard on her ass, she grips the back of the chair.

It doesn't hurt too badly; I have stronger toys I could have used. But the mixture of softness and sharpness is what makes her start to tremble.

As I keep teasing her, she slips her hand between her legs and begins to touch herself.

I let her.

I want to see her like this – giving into every primal urge she has. All the things she has been telling herself she can't think about or want.

When I give her my cock, she licks and sucks as if she has never wanted anything more in her life.

She stops, panting, and looks up at me. "Please," she says. "Fuck me again."

I drop the flogger to the floor and move behind her, slamming her back onto my cock with a force that makes the chair scrape against the flagstones.

The chair topples over, but I grab her, keep her standing, lift her into my arms and take her back to the bed.

This time, I use the tips of my wings to tease her.

"They feel different to the flogger, don't they?" I whisper as I caress her nipples.

She sighs and her back arches up towards me. "They feel so good," she moans.

I move to her feet. I kiss them gently, then nibble at her ankles. She laughs. The sound surprises me, but when I look up and see her smiling, it does something else to me.

A feral urge to make her smile again grips my insides.

I kiss from her ankles all the way up to the inside of her thighs.

Then I hold her hands above her head and slide slowly inside her. She meets my eyes. The hatred has gone. There is only *want* there now.

She keeps staring at me as I move inside her. I watch as her lips part, and her pleasure builds.

As our bodies slap together, entwined, her legs wrapped tight around my waist, my body mirrors hers.

As she starts to come, I feel myself unravel.

She clings on to me as if I am the only solid thing in an ocean of storms.

I hold her, too.

And I keep holding her until we fall asleep.

TWENTY-EIGHT

Finn

Yarrow and I have been entrenched in our small hut on the outskirts of camp all day, plotting and planning. The excitement in the air is palpable. We allowed the Leafborne, Pen, to join us. I don't like the guy, but he has spirit, and now that the Leafborne have decided they will fight with us, I figure we should at least make them feel involved.

"Garratt says the elves have been putting out word through the city," I tell them, leaning back against the stack of grain sacks behind me.

Now that I'm making regular journeys into the city, confident I won't be seen, I've been bringing back supplies which is keeping everyone fuller and happier.

Yarrow yawns loudly, lighting a cigarette. It is full of dandelion weed, which smells terrible but puts him in a good mood. He crosses his ankles and leans back opposite me. Pen is the only one standing. He's looking at our makeshift table and the maps that we have spread out of the city and the citadel.

"We need to agree on a day and a signal. The Shadowkind who are working for the Sunborne in the city will watch for the signal, maybe smoke," I say thoughtfully, watching as Yarrow puffs on his cigarette. "When they see it, they'll join us to fight."

"Wouldn't it be better to take down Eldrion first?" Pen says, tapping the castle on the map. "Take him down, take control of the castle, then deal with the other Sunborne when we have a fortress."

Yarrow looks at me and quirks his eyebrows. "The kid's not wrong," he says, even though I think Pen may be older than Yarrow; the Leafborne age a little more gracefully than we do.

I bite my lip. "My plan was for the Shadowkind to start fighting back against the Sunborne while we take the citadel, but perhaps Pen is right. Yes," I say slowly, "we'll do it while they're sleeping. We'll take Eldrion in the castle. The Sunborne will know nothing about it."

"And you're still relying on your girlfriend as our star player?" Yarrow asks, offering Pen a rolled-up cigarette. Pen hesitates, then accepts it, probably because he thinks it's polite. When he lights it and takes a puff, he winces a little but then carries on.

His wings are orange, which means fire magic.

"You saw what she did in the tunnels," I tell him. "She's powerful."

"We're all powerful," Pen says. He's leaning back against the table now, the dandelion weed taking effect already, and he looks more relaxed. "I can give you numbers if you like – who has which elemental magic, how many of us there are. And you know," he says, "why stop with us? Why not send word to the outer villages? We aren't the only ones the Gloomweavers have raided over the past couple of years while Eldrion turned a blind eye. The Mountain-borne, the Waterweavers – they'd come and help, I'm sure. It means being a little more organised." He says this last bit pointedly, looking at me.

I'm teetering on the edge of being annoyed, but then decide to laugh instead and shake my head at him.

"You're right," I say. "I'm not a born leader. I'm not smart. I've never made plans like this before. I'm just doing what I think is right for my people."

Pen's expression softens. "Well, lucky for you, part of our schooling includes stuff like this."

"It includes how to take over the capital city of the kingdom?" Yarrow says sarcastically.

"No," Pen says. "It involves studying battles, manoeuvres. Not all of us study it, of course, but I chose to do that instead of questing."

"Questing?" Yarrow asks with a withering stare.

Pen stands a little straighter, his expression becoming firmer. "At one hundred and fifty years old, each Leafborne fae has a choice – they quest, which means going away for a year –"

"On a quest," Yarrow finishes, narrowing his eyes with a hint of humour in his voice.

Pen laughs, but it's tinged with annoyance. "Exactly," he says. "Or studying more, choosing something to research, become an expert in."

"And you're an expert in battle?" I ask.

"Yes," Pen says. "It was two hundred years ago that I studied, but I remember most of it."

I stand up and clap him on the shoulder. "Then I am very glad you're here," I tell him. "Let's talk more about this idea – first, getting the other fae involved in the city. How will this work exactly?"

We talk until the sun has disappeared and the forest is cloaked in darkness. I know Alana will be wondering where I am, and fretting about it. Since I revealed the extent of my ambitions, she's been watching me closely. Like she's worried I will go off and leap into battle without her.

If she's worried about her role in the fight, she has not showed it. She has showed only steely determination.

Pride blooms in my chest as I think of her.

I saw it in her from the very first moment we met – her strength, her power, how special she was.

She knew it too, deep down. But the fae she grew up with didn't appreciate her. They spent their time making her feel *less* instead of *more*. Making her shy away from her powers instead of leaning into them.

I was determined to right their wrongs.

And when she succeeds in killing Eldrion, and takes her place as queen beside me, she will finally see what I see.

She's starting to. It began in the tunnels when she freed us all and made Eldrion fuck her on the way out. But I want her to really see it. I want her to see what she could be if she was by my side in the citadel when the rest of Luminael crumbles and the power balance is restored to what it once was.

Around the campfire, Leafborne and Shadowkind are finally starting to mingle with one another. It has only taken five weeks, stuck here together in this small piece of the forest that we have claimed as our own.

Briony is sitting beside Raine, the pregnant Leafborne who I have asked to be kept out of harm's way when the fighting starts; she is to be one of our healers. Not a warrior, even though this clearly displeased her.

Maura meets my gaze as I cross the clearing. The campfire casts dancing orange shadows on her face, and her expression remains unchanging.

She does not wave or smile; that woman barely does either.

In fact, she seems perpetually suspicious and irritated. With everyone.

Her attitude to Alana is what annoys me the most. Despite everything, she still behaves as though *she* is the one with the power. Because she is an 'elder'.

I abhor labels and titles.

In the new world order, there will be none.

Certainly no elders, presiding over everyone as if simply

being alive longer gives you some kind of expertise that no one else has.

I do not stop to talk, but when Briony leaves a small group of dancing Shadowkind and heads away from the music, I slow my pace and allow her to catch up.

"It has been too long since we spoke properly," I say, looping my arm around her shoulders. "How are you, Briony?"

"It's nice of you to ask," she says, and part of me wonders whether she is berating me for not checking in on her sooner. Probably, I should have. A good friend would have. But I have had too many other plates to juggle. "But before I answer you . . . have you seen Alana? She was missing from supper, and she's not by the lake." Briony stops walking.

I stop too and glance in the direction of mine and Alana's tent.

"I checked the tent, the lake, all her usual places. She sometimes walks for a long time, but something feels . . ." Briony wrinkles her nose. "I don't know, Finn. Something feels different. I'm worried she's gone beyond the shield."

"She can't." I frown. "I mean, she wouldn't. Why would she?"

Technically, the spell has been cast so that we can come and go as we please, and only those outside our group are prevented from being able to locate us. But why would Alana stray away from camp now, of all times?

Even as the thoughts form in my mind, a heavy weight settles deep in my stomach.

Quickening my pace, I march in the direction of the tent.

"Finn, I checked –" Briony is on my heels, hurrying to keep up.

I fling open the canvas and stoop inside. There. On the pillow. A note.

I scrunch it tight in my hand and wave it at Briony, allowing my anger to be directed at her. "You didn't see this?"

When she blinks at me, wide-eyed, clearly upset, I shake my head. My hands feel numb. "I'm sorry." I look at the piece of paper. I can't bring myself to open it. "I'm just worried she's done something stupid . . ."

Briony takes the paper from me and unfolds it. Her eyes scan the handwriting, and her face pales in the dim light of the tent.

"What is it? Where is she?"

"She's gone." Briony hands me the piece of paper. "Finn, she's gone to kill Eldrion."

My hands are trembling now. I look down through blurry eyes.

Dearest Finn,

Please do not be angry, my love. But I do not want you, or the others, to be put in harm's way. If you're right, and I have the power to end Eldrion, then it's something I should do alone. We have a connection. There is something that binds us, which gives me an advantage. But only if I go alone.

Please let me do this for you.

For all of you.

I love you, and I will see you on the other side. When the light returns to Luminael.

Yours always,

Alana

I meet Briony's eyes and allow the letter to flutter to the floor. "What has she done?" I whisper. "What the fuck has she done?"

TWENTY-NINE

Eldrion

I wake to the sensation of Alana springing from the bed, her face etched with horror as the realisation of what we've done seems to sink in. She paces the room, muttering to herself. With a flick of her wrist, she conjures an icicle back into her hand, the morning light glinting off its sharp edges.

Then she turns to me, holding it like a knife.

I try not to grin as I sit up, purposefully leaving the sheets draped so they barely cover the parts of me I know she'd like to see again up close.

I remain like that, tracking her movements. The air between us is charged, heavy with arousal, and despite the fury in her eyes – or perhaps because of it – all I want to do is drag her back into bed with me and hear her make those noises again.

Hear her call my name again, even if she does curse at me afterwards.

"Alana." My voice is still rough with sleep. "Please, listen to me. Let me explain. After, if you still choose to end my life, I won't stop you."

She pauses mid-stride, tension coiled in every line of her body. I can see the internal battle raging within her, the desire for answers warring with the anger and confusion that radiate from her in waves.

"I felt the same way you did. I needed answers, and I wanted you dead."

Her brow furrows. Is this a surprise to her?

"But I found answers. I know now why we are connected the way we are."

Slowly, as if every movement is a concession, she sits in the chair opposite the bed, plucking my robe from the back of it and wrapping it tightly around herself.

The dark fabric contrasts starkly with her pale skin and her purple wings, making her seem even more ethereal, more untouchable.

Fuck, it's good to see her wearing something of mine.

Why does the sight of it make me think of nothing but ripping it off her and devouring her again?

Her eyes meet mine. The icicle remains clutched in her hand, a tangible threat.

Would I let her stab me with it? If she truly wanted to kill me, would I allow her to?

Perhaps, because if she won't listen to me, then all is lost anyway.

"What I'm about to tell you . . . when you and I were last together, I had no idea *why* I needed you here. All I knew was that you were important to our future. I didn't know if you were to be trusted or whose side you were on."

"I'm on the side of people who don't torture and murder and kidnap innocent beings," she spits.

I blink at the venomous truth that spirals from her tongue. Like smoke, it curls around my ribs and squeezes.

That is how she sees me; a monster.

That is what I made myself.

"My mother . . ." I falter, the words sticking in my throat. The memory of reading those pages is still raw, still painful. I reach for the table beside the bed and Alana's entire body tenses.

The icicle looks both comical and intimidating in her hand. I want to remind her that I saw what she did to herself with one just like that . . . less pointed. But still . . . by the waterfall. On the rock. When I watched her, and called her my *good girl*.

As if she knows what I'm thinking, she starts to blush. She adjusts the robe, and frowns at me. "What are you doing?"

I pick up my mother's journal and toss it so it lands in her lap.

"My mother did something to yours, long ago. When your mother visited her. It's all recorded in there. A journal that belonged to my mother. I recognise her hand. She wrote in a signature ink. It couldn't be anyone else's. It's real."

Alana glances down at the book, then flicks open the cover.

"The bit about you starts a few pages in," I tell her. "Seems my mother wanted a record of her madness."

I sit up fully, the sheets pooling around my waist. I run a hand through my hair, trying to gather my thoughts, to find the right way to explain the inexplicable.

"She cast a spell, a dark ritual, on your mother while she was pregnant with you. She . . . changed you, gave you the powers you have now." I see the shock register on her face, her eyes widening, her lips parting in disbelief. She is scanning the words while I speak. But I press on.

"She believed you were the key to saving our kingdom from the evil that threatens it. That your powers were a gift, a weapon, to be used against the coming darkness."

Alana holds up her hand to silence me. She is reading. Her lips move, and I follow them. I have read the entry so many times, I know exactly what she is whispering.

I have seen the face of our salvation. A child, born of a healer's womb, with the power to turn the tide against the coming darkness.

As soon as I saw the child, I knew who she belonged to.

Magdalena. The healer who came to me from the Leafborne clan after Raylon's death. She came unasked, and I remember wondering why someone would do such a thing. Make such a long journey out of pure kindness.

She spent days with me, making tinctures and singing me lullabies. She was kinder to me than I ever remember my own mother being.

Now I know it was fate who brought her to me.

Now I know why we spent so many hours talking, with her counselling me through my grief.

It was all for this. So the child growing in her belly could save us all.

I did not want to hurt her. Magdalena was sweet and kind, and clearly longed for the child she carried. But I did what I had to do. What fate had asked of me.

I found an ancient spell, a ritual of dark magic that would change the child forever, mould her into the weapon we so desperately need. The elves held the spell, of course. In their library. The price for taking it was one I am not willing to put on record.

I do not want it remembered.

But I do want a record of what I did to Magdalena. In case I was wrong.

In case, instead of saving us all, I condemned us.

Would you like to know how I did it? If you're reading this, I assume you would. Either because things have gone horribly wrong or horribly right.

It was easy, really.

I am the Lady of Luminael. Everything comes easily to me.

She had not visited for a while, but I sent word that I'd like to see her before her baby was born. She arrived, belly full and round, wearing a yellow headscarf and carrying a bunch of poppies.

I remember thinking how quaint it was that she would bring a lady a bunch of flowers.

I sniffed them and put them in a vase.

She seemed pleased that I liked her offering.

After our usual talk and walk around the grounds of the citadel, I suggested we retire to my study for tea.

And that is when I drugged her.

She didn't suspect a thing, and didn't notice the strange taste or colour of the water. She just drank and talked, hand constantly resting on her belly.

When she finally passed out, I took the empty cup from her fingers and set it down on the table.

Then, as she slept, I performed the ritual.

A drop of my blood.

A bead of my sweat.

I mixed them with the powder the spell dictated, then I filled a large glass syringe and injected it into the child growing within her womb. With this magic, and the dark words of the incantation, I shaped her and twisted her, until she was no longer a mere fae, but something more. Something extraordinary.

I created a magic that had never before been seen in our lands. Not like this.

I created an empath, born to absorb the magic of others, to wield it as her own.

The one who will save us from what is coming.

Alana.

I knew her name because Magdalena had already used it. She knew her daughter's name long before she was born. And she loved her long before, too.

I whispered that name as Magdalena left that day, completely unaware that everything had changed for both her and her child.

Magdalena's child, Magdalena's flesh and blood, but my creation. My hope.

When Alana reaches the end of the passage, a tear rolls down her cheek.

"The visions," she whispers. Her grip on the icicle loosens slightly, and for a moment, I see a flicker of something else there, something that might just be understanding.

I nod, leaning forward intently. "They're not just dreams, Alana. My mother had them too. Perhaps my brother, as well. But he died too soon. And they passed to me."

"And then to me." She meets my gaze. She's put the icicle down now, and is holding the book with both hands instead. "When we . . . in the tunnels."

"They're premonitions, warnings of what's to come if we don't stop it."

"It's real? All of it?" She presses her palm to her chest, and I know she's reliving them the way I do whenever I try to close my eyes without whisky.

"And you." I meet her gaze. "You are the one destined to prevent it. That's why you can absorb magic, why you're so powerful. Why you're the only empath in centuries to possess these powers."

She's silent for a long moment, processing my words. She stands, icicle in one hand, journal in the other, and paces. Up and down. Up and down.

She pauses by the window and reads some more.

I can almost see the gears turning in her mind, the pieces of the puzzle falling into place. The icicle begins to melt in her hand, dripping onto the floor.

"Why didn't you tell me this before?" she asks finally, her voice barely above a whisper. "Why keep it from me?"

I sigh, running a hand over my face. "I didn't know, not until I found my mother's journal."

I rise from the bed, aware of my nakedness because she appraises my body even though she doesn't mean to. I cross the room to her.

"I know it's a lot to take in." I have never spoken to her like this before. In fact, I don't remember the last time I spoke to anyone like this. With softness instead of command.

She flinches slightly as I touch her arm but doesn't pull away. "But I need you to understand. Everything I've done, everything I've told you . . . it's real. I don't know when the demons are coming, but I know they are coming. And I know *you* are the only one who can stop them."

Alana looks down at the puddle of water on the floor, the remnants of the icicle she conjured. Then she meets my gaze again.

"I don't know if I can trust you," she says, tipping her chin up, fire blazing in her eyes. "After everything that's happened, everything you've done . . ."

"I've given you every reason to doubt me, to hate me. I am not a good man, Alana. I will not pretend to be. But I do speak the truth."

She's silent for a long moment, searching my face.

Then she shakes her head. "No," she says. "I don't trust you. How can I?" She throws the journal to the floor and storms away from me.

But I close the gap between us and grab her arm.

When she turns, she looks at me with pure fury in her eyes,

and I love how much she hates me. I deserve that hatred. My family deserves it. I want more of it.

She jerks away from me and starts picking up her clothes, shaking her head. "You're evil," she says. "You're trying to manipulate me."

I pull on my pants, fasten my belt, and stride towards her.

When I reach her, I squeeze her face tight between my thumbs. "Do you despise me so much, Alana, that you think I would lie about this?"

She tries to jerk away, but I hold her steady.

I lower my voice. "Do you despise yourself for wanting me?"

Her breath quickens, her skin shimmering in the early morning light that has begun to creep up over the horizon and through the cracks in the shutters.

This time, she does pull away from me. She strides over to the windows and throws open the shutters. "Look at my face," she barks. "See in the daylight just how much I *despise* you, Lord Eldrion."

I spread out my wings and stride towards her. I am bigger than her, stronger than her. And yet, she is stronger than me in a million other ways.

It makes me want to worship her and own her at the same time.

"On your knees, Leafborne." I tower over her.

She looks up at me, eyes glistening.

The torment that lights up her body is almost visible on

her flushed skin. Her lips part. I am hard for her already and I have not even touched her yet.

"On your knees," I repeat the command.

"No," she says. "On yours." She rises into the air and presses down on my shoulders.

To my surprise, I obey her.

When I am kneeling, she descends back to her feet, then leans back against the window, parts her legs, and rests one of them on my shoulder.

I grin, looking up at her from between her legs, then very gently reach out to touch her clit. She shivers as I make contact with her, and her sigh fills the room.

I lean in and bite the inside of her thigh, hard.

She gasps, but it is chased by a moan of pleasure, and she applies pressure to the back of my head, urging me to do it again.

I oblige, biting harder this time, and sucking until her skin grows darker beneath my teeth.

Jerking my head back, she pushes me away, turns around, and presses her palms against the window, presenting herself to me. I lick from her pussy to her ass, groaning as the taste of her fills my mouth.

Then I fuck her.

I slide into her waiting cunt effortlessly, and thrust hard.

I press down on her wings with one arm, causing her to whimper with discomfort but lean into it at the same time. "Please," she breathes. "Fuck me harder."

With my other hand, I grab her hip and pull her back onto me. She grinds them as I thrust, and continues to press her palms against the glass.

When she reaches down to play with her clit, her moans grow louder.

Our bodies slam together. Her walls tighten around me.

She punches the glass with a closed fist, and a splinter appears. I grin and fuck her harder.

She presses her palm onto the crack in the glass, then braces her other hand on the window too, so she can push back harder. And harder.

I stop, withdrawing my cock so only the tip remains inside her. Then, when she looks over her shoulder and says, "Don't stop," I slam back into her.

This time, the glass shatters.

We tumble forward, bodies locked together. I wrap my arms around her waist, beat my wings, and hold us there. Suspended in the air above the courtyard. Then I spin her around and fly us to the top of the castle.

Reaching back, I whip my belt from my pants and curl it around her wrists, then I tie her to the spire above my quarters.

When she is fixed there, I let go of her.

She is suspended, hundreds of feet above the ground. Of course, she could fly if she had to, but the adrenaline that course through her body is palpable.

I beat my wings, allowing the cool air to torment her naked body.

Her nipples peak, she arches towards me, searching for my touch, and her eyes blaze with fury.

“I could end you now, if I wanted to,” I murmur.

“You do not want to end me, or I’d have been dead long ago,” she replies, shifting her hips as arousal spreads down her inner thighs.

“What do you think I want from you, Alana?” I am close to her now, so close I can feel her breasts pressed up against my chest. I moisten one finger and use it to pinch her nipple. Her eyes widen. “Why would I lie to you about what you are? About what our visions are?”

“I have no idea why you’d lie, and I have no idea what you want with me.” She searches my face. “My powers? My body? All I know is that I can’t trust you.”

“You’re right about one thing.” I thrust my hand between her legs and apply pressure to her cunt. “I want your body, and I love that you give it to me so freely even though you cannot stand me. But you are not right about the rest. I meant it when I said you’re special. Everything I told you is true.”

“Stop talking.” She tilts her pelvis down, grinding onto my hand. “Stop talking and fuck me, Eldrion.”

“No.” I take my hand away. “I don’t think I will.”

Her eyes flash with rage. “What . . .?”

“I think I’ll leave you here, so you have some time with your own thoughts. So you can ruminate on whether I really am the bad guy or whether you believe what I’ve told you.”

"You wouldn't dare." She wriggles against the restraints that are holding her in place.

I meet her eyes. "Watch me."

When I return to my chambers, I am shaking. Did I really leave her up there? The thought is both exquisite, erotic torture, and terrifying.

What if I lose her again?

What if I'm playing a dangerous game and I'm about to lose?

My aim is to give her time to think, and then prove she can trust me when I return to her. But what if I've misjudged it? My mind is so clouded by lust for her and the need for her to believe me that I have no idea whether I'm doing the right thing.

I *feel* like the old version of me; the one who was cool, and calculated, and knew exactly what games to play and how to play them in order to get what he wanted.

But that does not mean I'm right.

I sink down into the chair by the broken window. The sun is only just rising. I reach for the whisky, then change my mind and set it down again. Instead, I pick up my mother's journal. And while I wait for the right moment to retrieve Alana, I read her words again. And again. And again.

I speak them loudly enough that they carry up in the air towards Alana.

I know she can hear them.

And I know that all she can do in this moment is listen.

THIRTY

Kayan

I am curled beside Rosalie. She cannot feel me or hear me, but I tell myself that perhaps I am giving her some comfort.

She cried for hours after her husband left. The fact he is her husband makes me sick to my stomach, and I know that shouldn't be possible.

I hate him.

That shouldn't be possible either.

And I know now that as soon as I see Alana, I need to ask for her help. She is powerful. She has magic that the Shadowkind believe can destroy Lord Eldrion, so she sure as hell can help me free Rosalie from this hell she's living in.

I have never blamed Alana for what happened to me. I didn't blame her for my death, or for my powers being taken. But if I have to use those things as leverage to make her help me, by the stars, I will.

Watching Rosalie cry, I wondered whether the spirit realm had made a mistake. Alana seems to be doing a perfectly fine job of guiding herself, so perhaps they were wrong. Perhaps I was meant to come back for Rosalie. Not Alana.

I know that's not true. I feel it, like a lead weight, in the pit of my stomach. Even though she told me to go, I am Alana's guide. But there is nothing in the rules that says I can't help Rosalie, too.

If there was, I wouldn't be here. They wouldn't let me.

I am watching Rosalie fall into a fitful sleep when something snags in my mind. A tugging sensation that pulls me upright and makes me shiver from head to toe. Alana?

It can't be. If she was calling me, I'd hear her voice.

But something isn't right.

I stand and walk over to the window. I don't want to leave. Rosalie is clutching the torn pieces of the sketch that her husband destroyed. I never knew she could draw. All the years we've known each other, and loved each other, and I never saw that piece of her.

We did not have enough time.

I look out at the expansive grounds of the house Rosalie now lives in. The old Sunborne fae bought her at auction for a reason, and although I'm not letting myself think about it – I know exactly what it was.

He needs a mother for his children.

She is to be lady of the manor house, but nothing more than a paid breeding mare for his pleasure. Paid in the trappings of an extravagant life.

This is what I thought Eldrion wanted with Alana when we were first taken – when he gave her chambers instead of locking her in the cellar with the rest of us. I was wrong. He wanted her for what she is, and because he was seeking answers to questions that sit heavy in his heart.

When he killed me, I saw a flicker – just a small flicker – of doubt in his eyes.

I remember it clearly because I thought he might change his mind. He hated me in that moment, but that wasn't the reason he was killing me. He hated me *because* he had to kill me.

He is not the same as the man who owns Rosalie.

Yes, Alana fucked him – although she thinks I don't know about it. But she wanted to. In all their secret meetings, he never once forced himself on her or made her do anything she didn't want to do.

All they did was talk.

I turn away from Rosalie and close my eyes. When I open them, I am down in the garden by a resplendent fountain. I stare at it, watch the water pooling in the basin.

I want to send her a message. I could . . . I could send a stream of water to batter her window. I could write in dew drops on her mirror.

I could tell her I'm still here.

But what if I'm not?

If Alana's journey comes to an end, and mine does too, Rosalie would lose me twice. Better for her not to know that I am watching her.

Better for her to think I am gone, and learn to live without me, than believe there's a fraction of hope that we could be together again one day.

I dip my hand into the fountain. I cannot feel the water. I miss it so much my heart hurts.

"Is there an instruction manual somewhere?" I ask, shaking my head as I sit down on the lip of the basin. "Something that explains what I'm allowed to feel and what I'm not allowed to feel? What these messages mean?"

I sigh and pinch the bridge of my nose.

I told Alana not to trust *them* and yet I have no idea who *they* are.

I am not in charge of the messages I am passing to her, and I cannot explain why or how that is the case.

No wonder she is furious with me; I am furious, too.

Except, I'm not. Because – like everything else – the fury is hidden beneath a blanket of cloud. Muted. Not quite there.

I am staring into the water, trying to persuade myself to move further away from Rosalie instead of sitting outside her window all night, when the same urgent sensation tugs in my gut.

This time, I know it has to do with Alana.

I look up at Rosalie's bedroom one last time, then whisper a promise that I will return, and feel myself disintegrate into the air.

When I reappear, I'm in the middle of the forest encampment, and everything is in complete chaos. Briony and Finn are shouting at one another. The fire in the middle of the camp is dwindling; no one is taking care of it.

Yarrow, the Shadowkind with the large beard, is pacing up and down, shaking his head. By a tall, twisted tree, Pen and Raine are watching, muttering something.

I move towards them and listen carefully.

"What was she thinking?" Pen shakes his head. "She's going to get us all killed. Eldrion will capture her again, force her to tell him where we are, and . . ."

"Don't say that." Raine folds her hands over her rounded stomach and sniffs. She looks like she's going to cry. Pen puts his arm around her and hugs her tightly.

"Don't cry, my love." He kisses her forehead.

He is not the father of her child, but clearly they have become close since our capture and her husband's death at the forest moon celebrations.

The night the Gloomweavers came for us.

"What's happening? Where's Alana?" I speak, but of course, no one answers, and I can't show myself to them. It would cause even more chaos, more questions.

I move towards Finn and Briony.

"I have to go after her." Finn looks completely panicked, and the expression on his face makes me doubt whether I was right not to trust him. I thought he was using her. I didn't like the way he spoke about her to Yarrow and the others. But there is no pretence now; he is distraught.

"This is my fault," he mutters. "I should never have let her think she could fight him alone."

Briony clasps Finn's hand between hers and squeezes tight. "This isn't your fault, Finn. It really isn't."

Finn shakes his head and pulls away. "Yes," he says. "It is. And I need to put it right."

Storming over, face like thunder clouds, Yarrow booms, "What now, Finn? You've lost her. Our one hope."

"She might do it," Briony says meekly. "You know how strong she is. You *wanted* her to do this."

"Not without backup," Finn says. "Not without a plan."

"She is a foolish woman." Yarrow folds his arms in front of his chest, and Finn instantly squares up to him.

"Say that again," he barks.

Yarrow stares down at him, then softens a little. "Finn," he says calmly. "You know I don't like Alana. Now is not the time to fight about it. Are you going to fetch her back or not?"

I hover between them, studying Finn's face. He doesn't hesitate for even a full second, just ducks into his tent, grabs his cloak, and says, "Fuck, yes. I'm going to get her back."

He is on the edge of the encampment when Briony catches him up. "If you're going, I'm coming with you." She puts her hands on her hips. She is short, and a little round, and her wings are small. She is no fighter. But she loves Alana.

Finn looks like he's about to object, but instead he inclines his head, and steps through the shield, extending a hand to pull Briony with him. "Come," he says. "Let's go."

I am about to go with them when a flicker of movement behind me in the bushes makes me turn around. Maura is staring straight at me.

She walks slowly forward, bare feet not making a single sound as they meet the damp forest floor. She stops in front of me, her eyes looking at me but through me at the same time.

"You can show yourself now," she says. "I think it's time we talked."

My body starts to tremble. The magic inside me flickers with the desire to follow her command, the desire to be seen.

"Kayan." This time, she says my name. "I know you're there, boy. And I'd like to see you now so we can talk about how to save Alana."

I close my eyes and take a deep breath. My blue light shimmers and glows. I watch my body materialise.

Maura takes a step back and blinks slowly at me. "Well," she says. "It's been a while since I saw a spirit. You look good."

I frown at her.

"Don't look so worried," she says. "You won't be in trouble."

"How do you know –"

"I've been alive a long time. When my husband died, he returned to me for a while. Vague messages, there to guide me . . ." She sighs and bends down to pick a blade of long grass. She starts to chew it. "It wasn't easy for him or me, and in the end, it proved no use."

"What was he supposed to guide you in?" I ask, watching as her thin jaw crunches down on the grass.

"That's another story for another time," she says. "My point is, the spirits don't always get it right. Sometimes their meddling is . . ." She shrugs. "Exactly that . . . meddling."

"But Alana . . ."

"Alana does need your help, yes." Maura turns and beckons for me to follow her. She sighs heavily as she walks. "I should have taken it all more seriously." She shakes her head. "Foolish fae."

"Taken what more seriously?"

When she stops, she's a few paces away from the fire. She stays in the shadows, speaking in a low voice so the others don't hear her talking to herself. "The message Eldrion's mother left when she came to tell us what Alana really was."

Something is building in my stomach. A sense of unease. The spirits aren't happy. This is not information I was supposed to have.

"What message?"

Maura drops the blade of grass and turns back to me. "She told me Alana was going to save us from the coming terrors of the world. That she created her. Imbued her with empathic magic when she was in Magdalena's belly and left her with us to be protected until the day the earth needed her." Maura bites her lower lip. "I think that day is now."

"But you hated her." I step in front of her, squaring my shoulders, anger pressing its whispering lips against the inside of my skin.

"I never hated her," Maura snaps. "I was afraid of her. I didn't trust the Lady of Luminael, and I didn't trust the Sunborne. And I *don't* trust empaths." She spread her wings and they flutter with annoyance. "I was waiting for Alana to prove herself. But every time I thought I knew what she was, something else happened." She meets my eyes. "But that is the past now."

"You believe she is to be trusted now?"

Maura wrinkles her nose and tucks her silver hair behind her ear. "I don't know. But I believe we've run out of time for guessing games." She points to the shield, the spot where Finn and Briony crossed through it. "We should follow them." She meets my eyes. "Are you with me?"

I nod firmly. "I'm with you."

THIRTY-ONE

Garratt

Elodie rearranges her skirts and wipes her lips. I smile down at her. Fuck, she's beautiful when she's all flushed from her orgasms.

Annoying as hell, still, but beautiful.

"So, you're playing them?" she asks, hopping up onto the bar and swinging her legs.

"Get down from there. We're opening soon." I frown at her.

She waits a moment, then does as she's told.

"Of course, I'm playing them. You think I'm stupid enough to choose sides in this thing?" I pour her a mug of ale, then one for myself.

This time, she slides onto a barstool as she takes a sip of her drink.

"How long have you known?" she asks, eyebrows quirking with curiosity.

"My mother was a guardian of the library." I shrug. "She told me all its secrets. I've known this was coming since I was a boy."

"And that's why you don't give a shit about whether you live or die," Elodie says, nodding as if my entire personality has just suddenly begun to make sense to her.

"I guess so," I muse, downing half my drink. "Just all seems a bit pointless. Eldrion's mother saw the end of the city. Demons, fire, floods. She *saw* it. So, what the hell made her think she could stop it? Is that how these things work? She just gets a version of the future and then has the chance to stop it becoming reality?"

Elodie frowns at me. She's not the sharpest elf in the city, and I'm losing her. But I'm speaking more for my own benefit than for hers.

"Orrr," I say, biting my inner cheek. "Is that the point? It's fated to be that way, and every step she takes – any of us takes – is simply drawing us closer to the inevitable conclusion."

"Which is?" Elodie frowns.

"Death." I shrug, laughing, even though she looks alarmed. "If you believe in fate, and believe fate has already decided, then that vision is going to come to life no matter what she did to try and stop it."

"What did she do?" Elodie taps her fingernails on the bar. "You haven't actually explained. You're talking in riddles."

I sigh and tilt my head. I'm unsure whether I completely trust her, but I figure the end is fast approaching so does it really matter? She's not stupid enough to betray me to

Eldrion or Finn at this point; she has too much to gain by being at my side.

"Eldrion's mother *created* the empath Eldrion has been seeking. She made her what she is because she thought she'd grow into this powerful being capable of stopping the demons from killing us all."

"What demons?" Elodie asks.

I shake my head and shrug. "The ones from the vision, I suppose." This part, I can't trust her with. I'm not even sure I trust *myself* with this part.

"But Finn and Eldrion both want Alana? The empath?" Elodie's voice has become a little nasal. It's because she's thinking.

"Finn wants her to kill Eldrion. Eldrion wants her to kill the demons."

"So, why doesn't Eldrion just tell Finn about the demons?"

I frown at her. "Because Finn . . ." I shake my head. "You know what, that's a good question. I'll suggest it to him next time I see him."

Elodie smiles. She actually thinks I'm serious. By the stars, I need to find someone new to fuck. Someone who can hold a conversation about something other than ale or runes.

"What of the Gloomweavers?" she asks, raising her eyebrows. "Is Eldrion going to allow them back into the city?"

I stare at her for a moment, then release a deep chuckle and shake my head. "Elodie, I don't actually *want* the

Gloomweavers back in the city. You'd be mad to want them back here."

"But you told Eldrion . . ."

"I needed to make him think I wanted something from him."

"But you don't?"

"All I want is for him to think I'm his friend, so that if he wins the fight, I become a confidant. Someone he trusts and bestows with a little of his great power." I shrug. "And I want the same from Finn. If he succeeds in killing Eldrion, he'll remember me as the one who helped him do so. And I'll –"

"You'll become his aide, someone he trusts . . ." Elodie rolls her eyes. "Okay, I got it now."

"You did?" I ask, trying not to show her the surprise I'm feeling.

She bites her lower lip and leans forward so her breasts swell beneath her tunic. "I'm not just a pretty face, you know," she coos.

Oh, but she is. Just a pretty face.

"Of course not," I tell her, meeting her lips over the bar and kissing her deeply. When I cup her face and draw a line with my other hand down between her breasts, I whisper, "You're one of the smartest women I know."

Elodie blushes and grins at me. "And you're one of the smartest guys I know."

Leaping over the bar, I pull up her skirt and bend her over

it. I slap her ass, then lean down and bite it. She likes that. It makes her squeal and wriggle back towards me.

As I fuck her, she calls my name, and the patrons wait patiently outside for me to unlock the doors.

I grab her hair and smile to myself.

I am smart.

I'm running this city, and neither Finn or Lord Eldrion have any fucking idea.

Long may it continue.

THIRTY-TWO

Finn

When we reach the tavern, there is a crowd outside. I push my way to the front, Briony close on my heels.

I do not care if I'm recognised. I need Garratt to open the fucking door.

I pound my fist hard on the wood. Behind me, someone shouts, "He's busy. Can't you hear?"

Pressing my ear to the door, I hear muffled cries from within. He's screwing someone. That's why he's making everyone wait out here?

"Garratt, open up!" I yell. "It's important. Open the hell-damned door!"

The noises stop. There's a shuffling sound, then the door flings open. Everyone files inside as Garratt holds the door open, and when they have passed him, I grab him by the collar and drag him outside. "We have to go," I tell him.

Shrugging out of my grip, Garratt straightens himself up. A female elf appears from inside. She is adjusting her skirt. "Everything all right?" she asks, staring at me, taking in my wings, and the bells on their tips, then biting her lower lip.

"Fine," Garratt says. "Just having a word with an old friend."

"I need you to get us into the castle." I close the gap between us. I am taller and more menacing but Garratt doesn't flinch.

"The castle? You're starting already?" He lowers his voice. "Finn, I thought . . ."

"No. Not for that." I am struggling to speak fast enough and clear enough. Briony steps in and speaks for me.

"Alana has gone to the castle to kill Lord Eldrion. Alone. We need to stop her."

Garratt's eyes widen. Something flickers in them as he looks at Briony, and Elodie notices it too because she slips her hand into Garratt's.

He shakes his head. That was not what he expected to hear, clearly. Then, without hesitating, he gestures to the stable yard. "We'll take my horses," he says. "Elodie –"

"I'm coming." She squeezes his hand. He looks at it with disdain but doesn't let go.

"Fine," he says. "You too?" He is looking at Briony.

"She's with me," I tell him, following quickly as we hurry into the yard and choose two grey horses. As I jump on, I pull Briony up beside me.

Garratt does the same with his elf girlfriend, and we canter out of the yard.

We travel through the streets of Luminael without stopping. When we reach the stretch of beach that leads out to the citadel, it is low tide. The water is too high for passing on foot, but not too high for the horses. So, we carry on.

When we reach the castle, Garratt turns to me. "Why would she do that?" he asks. "Go alone?"

"Because I told her she was capable of killing Eldrion." I swallow hard. Briony pats my shoulder.

"It wasn't your fault," she says. "Alana is headstrong. She'd have done it regardless of what you said."

I know that's not true, but I am grateful to her for saying it.

As we approach the castle gates, I pull my cloak tighter around my face, making sure my wings are hidden. Briony does the same beside me. We can't risk being recognised, not now.

Garratt takes the lead, striding up to the guards with a confidence that borders on arrogance. "Open the gates," he demands, his voice ringing out across the courtyard. "I have urgent business with Lord Eldrion."

The guards exchange a glance, then the larger of the two steps forward, his hand resting on the hilt of his sword. "The lord is not receiving visitors," he says gruffly. "And he certainly isn't expecting any elves."

Garratt's eyes narrow, and for a moment, I think he's going to argue. But then he smiles, a smile that doesn't quite reach his eyes. "Ah, but he is expecting me. I have information for him, information about the escaped prisoners."

The guard hesitates, uncertainty flickering across his face. "Wait here," he says finally. "I'll send word to the lord."

He turns to go, but Garratt's voice stops him. "No need for that," he says smoothly. "Just fetch Pria. She'll vouch for me."

The guard frowns, but nods to his companion. The other guard disappears into the castle, leaving us waiting in tense silence.

Beside me, Briony shifts uneasily. "Who's Pria?" she whispers.

"One of Eldrion's guards," I murmur back. "Garratt must have some sort of arrangement with her."

Before Briony can respond, the guard returns, a tall, dark-haired female fae at his side. Her wings are small, her features sharp and angular. She looks at Garratt, then at Elodie, and something like recognition flickers in her eyes.

"Garratt," she says, her voice cool and measured. "What brings you here?"

Garratt steps forward, lowering his voice. "I need to speak with Lord Eldrion. It's about the empath, Alana. She's coming here, and she means to kill him."

Pria's eyes widen, and for a moment, I see a flash of fear in their depths. Then her expression hardens, and she nods curtly. "Come with me," she says. "Quickly."

. . .

She leads us through the gates into the courtyard beyond. I keep my head down, my heart pounding in my chest. I can feel the eyes of the guards on us, suspicious and wary.

I recognise some of them. Just a few weeks ago, we were kin. Now, they are the ones who stayed and I am the enemy who fled.

Pria's presence seems to be enough to grant us passage, and we make it into the castle without incident.

Once inside, Pria turns to face us, her eyes flicking to me and Briony. "Who are they?" she asks Garratt, her voice tight with suspicion.

"Friends," Garratt says simply. "They're here to help."

Pria looks like she wants to argue, or ask why we feel it necessary to hide our faces, but then she shakes her head. "Fine. But if they cause any trouble, it's on you."

She leads us through the winding corridors of the castle, her steps quick and purposeful. Being back here is like coming home, and the very fact I feel that way sends jolts of despair to the pit of my stomach.

Everything is familiar. The smells, the sounds, the way the air feels.

Finally, we emerge into a large, circular room. The banquet hall. I look up at the ceiling. The remains of my very last act still hang from the rafters.

"All right." Pria puts her hands on her hips. "Time for the truth, Garratt." She jerks her thumb at me and Briony. "Who are they and what is going on?"

Squaring my shoulders, I push the cloak from my face and extend my hand. "I don't think we ever met, but I remember you."

Pria stares at me for a second, then shakes my hand. "The jester," she says. "You've returned?"

I shake my head. "Garratt was telling the truth. But Alana is not *coming* here. She is already here."

"That's impossible." Pria folds her arms in front of her chest. "I'd know if there was someone here."

"Have you seen Eldrion today?" Briony asks, taking off her own hood.

When Pria sees her, she smiles. Clearly, they do know each other because they embrace and hold contact for a little longer than necessary. "Not today, no," Pria says as she steps back. "But there's no way Alana could have gotten in here without the guards knowing."

"What if she used the tunnels?" I ask.

"They collapsed when you escaped. It's simply not possible."

"Alana is capable of more than you know." I gesture to the doors. "Take me to Eldrion."

Pria hesitates. "Finn . . . if he catches you here."

"Alana is about to get herself killed," I snap. "And I am not going to let that happen. You can help me or you can stand aside, like you did when we escaped this wretched place. Either way, I'm going to find Alana."

My words have hurt her. I can tell by the way her gaze softens and she shuffles her feet. "Very well," she says. "I'll take you to him. But we have to cross the courtyard. He had the stairs to his chambers sealed. The only way in is via the spiral staircase on the outer wall."

I extend my arm and nod at her. "Then, lead the way."

THIRTY-THREE

Alana

I have no idea how many times Eldrion reads his mother's journal to me.

He reads it from start to finish, every single word. As I listen and try to truly absorb what they mean, it occurs to me that suddenly, with these words, my entire life makes sense.

I never understood what I was or why I was.

I never understood why the people around me hated me so much, or why there was no one to teach me how to use my magic. But it was because I should never have existed – not the way I do now.

I am unnatural, a thing that was created of magic and for magic.

I was a pawn in a bigger game even before I took my first breath, and I think of how many lives have been ruined because of it, because one fae who had a vision decided that she could stop the inevitable.

Eldrion pauses. He's about to turn the page when I call down to him, "I have a question."

I hear his bare feet on the floorboards, and then I see him fly from the window up to join me.

He takes in my naked form, looks at my wrists, which are sore from the amount of time they've been bound to the steeple, even though my wings have been keeping me afloat and taking some of the pressure off them.

"I have a question, and I want to talk to you, but I will not do it like this."

He nods at me, then wraps his arms around me and carries me to the roof.

After setting me down, he leaves me alone, returns to his room, and comes back carrying his robe.

He wraps it around me with a surprising amount of care. In fact, everything about his movements is suddenly slow and soft, and it's almost as alarming as when he is hard and callous.

I catch myself breathing in the scent of him as I pull the robe closer, then berate myself.

I am standing here, on the spot where he held Kayan and forced us all to watch. And I am thinking about how good his *robe* smells against my skin.

Looking down, I wonder if he is thinking of Kayan the way I am. I wonder if he is remembering the moment when he killed my best friend.

But that is not what I want to ask him about. "The visions." I turn to him and meet his eyes.

Looking into them is difficult because when I do, I see a mixture of lust and hatred that drives me wild.

My body responds to him even when my mind doesn't want to. I pull the robe tighter around my body and pace away, putting some distance between us.

"Yes," he says, tucking his silver hair behind his ear. At least he's wearing pants, so I'm not distracted by the piercings that drive me wild when they're inside me.

I force myself to look at him as I ask the question because I want to see the expression on his face when I ask it.

"They are premonitions, yes? So, how do we know we can stop them? You tell me your mother created me because she believed I could stop what's coming. What if I'm part of it? What if this whole thing has just led us to the point where it's going to happen anyway?"

I expect him to answer me quickly with a rebuttal, but instead, he frowns.

I can almost see the wheels turning in his mind as he thinks.

He bites his lip, rubs his chin, the back of his neck, and his large black wings twitch.

"Honestly," he says, "I do not know."

I study his face and then part my lips. "You don't know? All of this –" I stretch my arms out wide and then point to the spot where he dropped Kayan to the floor like a disused toy – "all of this death and destruction, the people you've hurt, the things you have done, and you don't know?"

As he looks at me, something in his expression changes, as if he's sad that I am disappointed in him.

Anger, he can cope with; that makes him hard enough to fuck me into oblivion. But disappointment or disdain, clearly that's different.

"All I know is what I've told you." He lifts the journal and taps its cover. "The information in these pages is new to me. Perhaps if I'd had it sooner, I would've had time to interrogate it further, to think about the questions you're asking me, but I didn't." He's speaking quickly now, his tone darker. "I had no one to guide me growing up, Alana. My brother was supposed to be the ruler of Luminael, but he died. And by the time my mother died too, I still didn't have my powers. They emerged after all my family was gone. For years, I ruled with the threat of my powers when I had none. I lived in terror of being found out and losing control. And then, when they did arrive, I wished they hadn't. My mother never taught me how to interpret the visions because she never thought I would have to. My brother was supposed to be doing this, not me."

He turns away from me, and I wish he hadn't, because the way he looked in that moment, talking about his family, is different from anything I have seen on his face in the time we've known each other so far.

"My brother died too," I tell him. I don't know why I am telling him, but it makes him stop, breathing heavily, his wings moving at the same time as his shoulders, up and down. "Earlier than he should have," I say. "He died trying to protect me."

"Mine did the same for me," he replies when he turns around.

An unmistakable urge to be closer to him washes over me, and as soon as it does, it is chased by a tinge of guilt and then the familiar throb of anger.

"If it's true, and I am the one who will stop these demons from coming, stop the visions from happening. How am I supposed to do that?"

"I don't know." Eldrion braces his hands on the edge of the roof. He kicks the wall in a movement that's slightly comical, like a stroppy teenager who's not getting their way.

"So, I'm supposed to wait in this castle with you until it happens, and then what?"

"I don't know," he bites back. "Why are you so annoying?" He spins around and stares at me, and suddenly, I laugh. "Why are you laughing?" he asks, stalking towards me.

He grabs me by the waist and pulls, the robe falling open so that my naked chest is pressed against his.

"Because you called me annoying, and it's ridiculous," I tell him. "We are talking about the survival of an entire kingdom, and you think I'm annoying."

"You *are* annoying," he growls.

"You should probably shut me up, then, shouldn't you?" How do I even pretend I don't want him to kiss me?

Our lips collide, and his tongue enters my mouth as his hands roam my body, his wings enveloping me.

They feel the way they did last night. And somehow, wrapped inside them, as much as I hate him, I feel safe with him.

But then, something in the air changes. I push him away and stumble backwards.

Something is happening. Something is coming closer.

I try to latch onto it. The sensation is familiar.

I race to the edge of the roof and look down, and then I know what it was that I felt.

It was Finn.

I call his name three times, and finally, he looks up. He's with Briony and three other figures who I don't recognise.

"Alana," he calls, "whatever you're about to do, don't do it."

Eldrion is at my side now. He presses his hand firmly on mine. "Leave, jester," he calls. "You are not wanted here. Leave and I will let you live."

My heart freezes in my chest. I turn to Eldrion, but I remember what happened the last time I pleaded with him to spare someone dear to me, and stop before the words have passed my lips.

Below, Finn is not heeding Eldon's warning.

Ignoring him completely, he calls up to me, "I'm coming to get you, Alana. Don't worry, I'm coming."

THIRTY-FOUR

Maura

TWO HUNDRED AND FIFTY YEARS AGO

Phillipe has only been gone a week, but it feels like forever. I have been trying to remember a time before we met, and before I loved him. But it is impossible. Five hundred years, I've lived, and he has been by my side for nearly all of them.

Had been.

He is no more.

It's funny, I always thought he would live longer. My father reached six hundred and fifty. My mother a little more.

But the sickness sweeping through the village claimed him, and even the best healers couldn't stop him fading away.

In the end, I was glad for an end to his suffering. I

welcomed it for him. But I am sad for me, now, not for him.

I am sad that the reason I'm becoming an elder is because his position on the council became free. And I'm sad that he won't see me at the ceremony, receiving my bracelet of leaves and my staff.

As I stand and stare out at the sunset above the lake, I think of all the years I may have left in front of me and I think about going through them alone.

We had no children. It was not meant to be for us. And although the young fae of the village call me *auntie* and clamber into my cabin when they wake early and their parents tell them to go play, because they know I will tell them stories and bake them fresh bread, they are not *my* kin.

Slowly the sun appears above the crown of the trees on the other side of the lake. She is pale today, and a little sickly.

She reminds me of myself.

I look at my reflection in the surface of the lake. I am old. My skin is thin, and my bones protrude beneath it like daggers. I have always been angular, but age has made me more so.

It is why I am taken seriously.

Other females, softer females, struggle. But I never have.

I am listened to.

But what is the point of it if Phillipe isn't there to see it?

The look in his eyes when I stood up for myself, or for

another, and when I showed power or dominance, was always the thing that drove the passion in our marriage.

He worshipped me, and made me feel like the very best version of myself.

Although some arranged marriages are sad and lonely for both parties, and they have fallen out of fashion in recent years, ours was never like that.

He was everything to me.

Without him, my body feels empty and fragile, like I am waiting to be cracked open and trodden upon. My bones ground into the earth.

I look to the spot where his funeral pyre was just a few days ago.

It was a beautiful ceremony. There were songs, and laughter, and memories. It was exactly how it should have been. And I was almost happy because it felt as if he was there with me. It was *good* to be celebrating his life.

But then the celebration was over, and everyone else resumed their daily chores and duties and studies and ventures.

And I was left alone.

Floating through the forest like a spectre. Unable to engage in small talk or to take an interest in the goings-on of the council because it all feels miraculously pointless now that I have no Phillipe to go home to at night.

I know it is too early to feel like this.

I have to wade through my grief and, one day, I will come out the other side.

I have counselled many bereaved parents and siblings and spouses over the years. I know the platitudes off by heart.

But I do not believe they apply to me.

I am too old. I have seen too much. And I have no desire to 'come out the other side' for what is there for me when I reach it? Another great love? Friendship? Adventure?

I have experienced it all already, tenfold, and I do not need any more of it.

So, I wade into the water.

Behind me, the earth shakes a warning, and my wings flutter. But I lift the stones I have weighted to two large piece of rope and wrap them around myself, pinning my wings to my sides.

I walk forward, towards the spot where Phillipe's body was finally submerged into the lake.

I will join him, and we will be together, and the pain will stop.

"Auntie Maura, what are you doing?" a small voice floats towards me on the breeze, and before I can reply, Alana appears.

She is floating in the air beside me. Just eleven years old, but her wings are already larger than those of her peers. They are glowing purple. She stares at me and starts to cry.

"Oh," she says. "Oh dear."

She looks at the rope around my waist, and the stones that hang from it, and even though she is so very young, she understands in an instant what I am trying to do.

The look on her face brings me to my senses. As she sobs, treading air with her little purple wings, I struggle to free myself from the ropes. I let them fall into the water, then reach for her and bring her into my arms.

I wade back to the shoreline as she sobs against my chest.

"I am sorry, child. I did not mean to frighten you."

I set her down on the sand and sit beside her. My dress is soaked and clinging to my thin legs. She is wet too from being pressed against me.

She sniffs loudly and wipes her nose with the back of her hand. Her hair is unruly. Bright auburn and hanging loose around her shoulders.

Her sea-green eyes look even more green now they are tinged with tears.

"You miss him," she says.

I nod slowly and fold my hands into my lap. "Yes, my dear. I miss him."

"The sadness will go away, though," she says. "That's what they told me when my auntie died, and they were right."

I try to smile and reach for her hand. "Yes, I think you're right. It will."

"I can help." Alana turns her big eyes up at me and squeezes my hand. "I can make the sad go away for you, if you'd like me to."

My heartbeat trips in my chest. "Make it go away?" I frown at her and lean in closer. "What do you mean, my love?"

"Sometimes, when my friends are cross with me, I make it stop." She shrugs, and a sensation like ice-cold dread drips down my spine. She is so young, and she can already play with people's emotions like that?

"How do you make it stop?" I ask her, my mouth suddenly dry.

Alana shrugs. "I'm not really sure," she says. Her voice is so small, so sweet, so innocent. But the power of her words burns like acid on my skin. She has no idea what she is or how to control what she is, and we cannot help her.

There has never been an empathic Leafborne before; the other villagers don't even know what she is yet. We have kept it hidden from them, but if she starts talking like this to others, they will know. And when they know, they will feel the same way I am feeling now; like they're not sure whether they are looking at a demon or an angel.

"Alana, would you show me?" I inhale slowly.

I shouldn't ask it of her. Every fibre of sense in my body is telling me not to, but at the same time, I am desperate for the pain to go away.

So, I tell myself I am asking so I can try to understand what it is she does and whether it really is as dangerous as it feels.

"Of course, Auntie Maura." She smiles at me and takes my hands in hers.

Her wings start to flutter. Purple light surrounds her, dancing on her skin and floating from her fingertips towards me. As it reaches me, it turns from light to smoke. It surrounds me, pressing down on my skin with a warmth that feels endlessly comforting.

I close my eyes and lean into the sensation. I sigh, and as I open my mouth, the smoke fills it up. I feel it trickle down through my body. Warm water and sunlight. Cleansing me from the inside out.

I give myself up to the sensations. I hear Alana speaking, but I cannot focus on her words.

The warmth turns to heat. It grows and swells and then rushes from my body, tearing the breath from my lungs and making me fold forward onto my knees.

When I open my eyes, the smoke is surrounding Alana. It is darker now. A deep, thick shade of purple instead of bright happy violet.

Alana breathes it in. She coughs. Her little face grows red. And then she releases it.

The smoke swirls up into the air, and disappears. Disintegrates over the lake.

She collapses backwards, lying face up, arms at her sides.

I scramble over to her and shake her shoulders. She looks exhausted, and pale. Slowly, she turns her head towards me and smiles. "Did it work?" she asks quietly. "Did I help?"

I lie down beside her and cradle her beneath my wing. Her body is cold, and clammy. She is breathing unevenly.

Whatever she just did was dangerous for her.

"Alana, you mustn't do that again," I tell her.

"But it worked?" she asks.

"Yes, it worked." I press my palm to my chest, searching for the sadness that was so profound only a few moments ago.

It has gone.

But when I sit up, and stare out at the lake, I do not feel glad of it; I feel like a traitor to my husband's memory.

And when Alana slips her small hand into mine, I do not feel glad of her, either. I feel terrified. Because she *enjoyed* what she did.

And I have no idea whether it's because she wanted to help me or because she enjoyed having power over me.

For the first time since she was born, watching her skip away into the forest and call for her brother and her friends, I am truly afraid of what we have living in our midst.

And of what she will become.

THIRTY-FIVE

Eldrion

"Do not leave with him." I grab Alana's elbow and pull her towards me. "You know I have been telling you the truth, Alana. This is where you belong."

She meets my eyes. A few short minutes ago, I thought I had got through to her. But the confusion is back.

She grips the sides of her head and storms away from me.

"I can't think," she says, shaking her arms out at her sides as if it will remove the tension that is swirling through her body. "I need to think."

Footsteps sound on the staircase. They are drawing closer.

"I won't stop you." I stand back and lower my arms to my sides. "If you choose to go, I won't stop you or fight you."

She frowns at me and shakes her head. "Why would you do that?"

"Because I am trying to prove that you can trust me."

A laugh bursts from her lips, but it is not the happy laugh that I coaxed from her when we were fucking. It is an exasperated laugh. "I cannot even trust my own mind," she says. "I just fucked the man who killed my best friend. I came here to end you, and instead I –"

"Doesn't that tell you something?" I stride towards her, anger flaring in my eyes.

"It tells me I need this to be over," she says, scraping her fingers through her hair.

The footsteps have reached the door, now. Finn bursts onto the roof. He looks different. More self-assured now. And I know in an instant that his concern for Alana is an act.

How does she not see it? I turn to warn her, but she is already rushing towards him. He pulls her into his arms, then stands in front of her, motioning for her to leave.

Briony is with him and . . . "Garratt?"

The elf meets my gaze and shrugs. "Apologies, my lord," he says. "I'm sure you understand. Business is business."

He glances at his girlfriend, then shakes his head. "In fact, this is none of my business at all." He backs slowly away towards the door, but a burst of anger erupts inside me and I send a wave of power to slam it shut. "No one leaves!"

Alana turns her green eyes on me. "What happened to *you can leave if you want to*," she says, squaring up to me.

"I changed my mind." I glance at Finn. There is no way I'm letting him take her.

"Alana, don't." He makes a weak show of trying to hold her back, but ultimately does not stop her as she strides towards me, purple magic glistening in her palms.

"I need him gone," she cries, pulling her arm back and hurling a ball of violet light in my direction. I deflect it with ease.

"I don't want to fight you, Alana. But you have to see what he's doing. He's manipulating you."

"Says you!" she yells, throwing another ball of light.

"Alana, don't trust him," Finn calls. "Remember what he is and what his people have done. Remember all the things I showed you."

"What has he showed you?" I square my shoulders. We are circling each other now. How she thinks she can take me on, I do not know. She is not strong enough.

She flicks her wrist and, just like that, a dozen tiny icicles form in the air. She sends them hurtling towards me.

"You should have done that last night," I shout as I bat them away with a shield of shadow. "Before you decided to fuck me instead."

Alana stops dead. Her breath hitches. She glances back at Finn, and I use the moment to send a vortex of shadow towards her.

I do not want to hurt her. I just need to stop her from leaving, and make her see that I . . .

She ducks beneath the shadows, then summons some of her own. Except, these are purple and more like smoke.

"I might not be able to kill you," she says. "But I have no problem taking your powers from you."

She closes her eyes and tilts her head to the side. Her smoke draws closer, it creeps along the floor until it touches my toes. It is warm, and comforting. Not as I expected it to be.

I wait for a moment, transfixed, watching it wind slowly up my legs.

I try to kick it off, but it's no use.

This time, I do not hold back. My eyes roll back and become darker. My wings flare out to my sides, and I roar as I bring power and fury out of the shadows into the light.

Everyone else on the roof scrambles backwards. It is just Alana and me now. Circling each other like wild animals.

As her purple smoke winds its way up my body, I feel a strange sensation – a tugging, a draining. With a jolt, I realise what's happening. Alana is trying to take my magic.

I fight back, summoning every ounce of strength I possess. The shadows around me thicken, darkening to an inky black. They pulse with malevolent energy, straining against Alana's hold. I have not unleashed them like this before, but it is a power I always knew I had inside me.

I have never needed to use it. Until now.

But it's not enough. Her smoke keeps creeping, keeps pulling. I can feel my magic slipping away, drawn inexorably into her the way I am.

It is as if it needs to be inside her.

As I watch, visions of our bodies, entwined and naked, flash in front of my eyes.

I want her like that now. What if this all ended and we went back to that?

Desperate, I gather my shadows into a massive, roiling cloud. "Don't make me hurt you, Alana." I plead with her, meeting her eyes.

A few short hours ago, I saw flickers of warmth in her gaze. Even beneath the hate and the fury, I saw a part of her that wanted me. *Really* wanted me.

There was a place deep inside her that wanted to trust me.

But that place is unreachable, and if I don't act now, I will lose everything I am.

With a roar of fury and fear, I hurl my magic towards her, putting every last bit of my power behind it.

The cloud rushes forward, a tsunami of darkness. Alana's eyes widen, her concentration breaking. She throws up her hands, a shield of purple light forming before her.

But before the shadows reach her, a figure leaps in front of her.

Finn, his wings spread wide. He opens his arms, and takes the attack. The shadows hit his chest with a force that sends him flying. He hits the wall, and crumples to the floor like a ragdoll.

I cannot stop it now.

The shadows engulf him. For a moment, he is lost from view, swallowed by the darkness.

Alana screams his name.

I stare in shock, the shadows thinning. It could have been her. If I'd hit her . . .

I am shaking. I stumble backwards.

And then, as the darkness clears, I see him. Finn is lying motionless on the ground, his wings bent at an unnatural angle.

Alana rushes to his side, dropping to her knees beside him. She gathers him into her arms, cradling his head against her chest. Tears stream down her face as she calls his name, begging him to wake up.

But he doesn't move.

The jester is dead.

THIRTY-SIX

Alana

I drop to my knees, my heart shattering into a million pieces as I stare at Finn's lifeless body. His skin is deathly pale, almost translucent, and his once vibrant eyes are now dull and empty.

I can't breathe, can't think.

This can't be happening. Not like this. Not now.

"Finn . . ." I run my hands over his chest, desperately searching for any sign of life. "Please, please wake up. I'm sorry. I'm so sorry."

But he doesn't move, doesn't respond. His body is still.

Behind me, Briony approaches slowly. She puts her hand on my shoulder. "Alana," she sobs. "We should go." She glances to her left.

Eldrion is clinging on to the edge of the roof, back towards us, breathing heavily.

"Finn would want us to go," she pleads.

From the corner of my eye, I notice the elves and the Shadowkind guard disappearing down the steps back into the castle.

"I can't leave him." I turn back to Finn and cup his face in my hands. I brush my hand over his eyes, closing them, then kiss his forehead.

"Alana, please." Briony tugs my arm, but I jerk out of her grasp.

"You go. I'm not leaving."

"His wings . . ." It is Eldrion's voice. I look up, blinking through the tears that blur my vision.

Eldrion draws closer. I stand and splay out my fingers. "You will not touch him," I hiss.

"Alana, his wings." Eldrion points to Finn.

I look around quickly. At first, I don't notice what he's looking at. But then I realise that Finn's wings, once a dull, tattered grey, are now black. Pitch black, like the darkest night.

I look up, my eyes locking with Eldrion's. He stands there, motionless, watching me with an expression I can't quite read. Is it sorrow? Regret? Or something darker, more twisted?

I don't care. All I care about is Finn. My Finn, who jumped in front of me, who took the blow meant for me. Who sacrificed himself to save me.

I turn back to him, gathering him into my arms. His body is heavy, limp, and so, so cold. I bury my face in his neck, my tears soaking into his skin.

He's gone, and it's all my fault.

No. It's not my fault. It's Eldrion's.

When I stand, my grief and sorrow begin to morph into something else. Something hot and fierce and all-consuming.

Rage.

I turn to face Eldrion, my hands clenching into fists at my sides. Purple light begins to flicker around me, tendrils of energy that snap and crackle in the air.

"You," I hiss, my voice low and dangerous. "You did this."

"I did not mean for this to happen, Alana."

"You took Kayan and now you have taken Finn." I shake my head, the fury building inside me like a volcano ready to erupt. "No," I snarl. "This is on you. All of it. The suffering, the pain, the death. It's all because of you."

The light around me grows brighter, more intense. I can feel the power surging through my veins. "And now," I whisper, my eyes locking with Eldrion's, "you're going to pay."

I raise my hands, purple flames dancing at my fingertips. Eldrion's eyes widen, and for the first time, I see a flicker of fear in their depths.

Good. He should be afraid.

I take a step forward. But then, a sound cuts through the roaring in my ears.

A cough.

I spin around, my heart leaping into my throat.

There, hovering a few inches off the ground, is Finn.

His eyes are open, his chest rising and falling with shallow breaths.

He's alive.

But then I see his wings, still black as night. They are moving. They are growing.

I stagger backward and reach for Briony's hand. Finn's body rights itself so he is upright in the air. And his wings continue to grow.

His eyes spring open. He is staring at me. I jerk forward, but Briony keeps hold of me.

Finn tilts his head, then opens his mouth. A scream that makes my bones feel as if they might splinter fills the air. It grows louder, and louder.

A cracking sound follows it.

His arm jerks into an unnatural angle. Then the other arm, and his legs.

His body is breaking.

I cry out and drop to my knees. "What are you doing to him? Stop!" I turn to Eldrion, no longer too proud to beg.

But when he meets my eyes, the look I see on his face sends a shiver of dread to the very basement of my soul. "I am not doing this," he shouts over the sound of Finn's pain. Then, wrapping his wings around me, he pulls me back, grabbing Briony, too.

Eldrion stands in front of us. Shadows start to swirl around his fingers. But instead of flowing out, towards Finn, they begin to flow inwards. They coil around Eldrion's arm, and squeeze. He tries to shake them off.

In the air, suspended in front of us, Finn is watching. But his body continues to break.

Now, he is like a tortured marionette. Limbs hanging loose, held up by his enormous new wings.

He blinks. When he opens his eyes again, they are red, and his limbs begin to solidify once more. Only now, they are bigger. Stronger.

Shadows swirl around him, but they are not hurting him. They dance on his skin, leaving it decorated with ink-like patterns. The ink snakes up his throat, over his arms, onto his hands. Then the sides of his face, too.

A moment ago, his skin was completely free of blemishes. Now, it is covered in tattoos I cannot interpret.

Finn flexes his wrist. The shadows playfully float from his palm. "They do not listen to you now, Eldrion," he hisses. "They listen to me."

I turn and see Eldrion's eyes widening as the shadows press down upon him, squeezing his chest, constricting his ribs.

"They listen *only* to me, now." Finn shakes his wings. There is a familiar chime that almost brings a smile to my face, but then there is the sound of the bells falling to the floor.

I look down to see two jester's bells at my feet. When I look up, Finn is staring at me. "Thank you, Alana," he breathes. "I could not have done this without you."

I stagger backwards, clinging on to Briony.

"I meant what I said." Finn extends his hand for mine. "I want you to be beside me when I take the world back to how it was before."

He blinks at me again, and then I see it. The red eyes.

Red eyes glinting in a shadow-covered face.

I remember the vision I had in the woods. The demon that loomed over Eldrion and me. The way it laughed at us.

"You can do it, Alana, take his magic." Eldrion talked softly into my ear.

I remember the words. But I misunderstood them.

I thought Eldrion wanted me to take the demon's powers and give them to him. I was wrong. All this time, it was Finn who wanted *Eldrion's* power. And I gave him exactly what he wanted.

Waves of nausea wash over me.

I vomit onto the floor.

Finn tuts at me, then laughs. "Poor, sweet girl," he hisses. "I guess this means you won't be joining me after all?"

Behind me, Eldrion is gasping for breath. I turn away from Finn and bring flickering balls of purple light into my hands. I throw them at the shadows, and they dissipate like forks of lightning. I throw more, and more.

Finally, I break them. I yank Eldrion free and shake him. "Eldrion, you have to help me."

Finn rises up higher into the air. He seems unconcerned by us now. As if we are so small and insignificant that he will not waste another second thinking about us.

Briony rushes to the edge of the roof. Finn is above us. His wings stretch out, filling the sky. Shadows swirl around him like storm clouds. Thunder rumbles and lightning cracks. He pulls the shadows in around him, breathes deeply, then disappears.

He is gone.

But he is not finished with us.

This is only the beginning.

Epilogue

The Rise and Fall of the Shadowkind:
A Treatise on the Darkest Chapter of Our History

In the ancient annals of our kingdom, there exists a race of fae known as the Shadowkind. Born with wings as dark as night and hearts to match, these creatures were once the scourge of our realm, their very existence a blight upon the land.

It is said that in the early days, the Shadowkind lived amongst the other fae, their true nature hidden beneath a veneer of civility. But as they reached the age of fifty, a strange and terrible transformation would occur. Their wings, once small and unremarkable, would grow and mature, becoming vast and powerful. And with this physical change came a darkness of the soul, a corruption that twisted their very being.

The Shadowkind were beings of pure evil, their magic fuelled by the shadows that clung to their wings. They rampaged across the kingdom, spreading terror and destruction wherever they went. The other fae, the Leafborne, the Mountainborne, and Waterweavers, lived in constant fear, never knowing when the next attack would come.

In those dark days, the Sunborne lived apart, sequestered in their citadel like monks in a monastery. They were the guardians of light and, along with the elves, the keepers of ancient knowledge. But they did not interfere in the affairs of the outside world. And so, for generations, the kingdom suffered under the reign of shadows.

Until a hero arose from among the Sunborne. The first of the line that would become known as the Lords and Ladies of Luminael. This brave and noble fae, whose name has been lost to history, looked upon the suffering of the kingdom and knew that something had to be done.

With a small but devoted band of followers, he ventured forth from the citadel and took the fight to the Shadowkind. The war that followed was long and brutal, the forces of light and darkness clashing in a conflict that threatened to tear the very fabric of the world asunder.

But in the end, the Sunborne prevailed.

The Shadowkind were defeated, their armies scattered, their power broken. But the hero knew this was not enough. As long as the Shadowkind's wings remained unbound, as long as their dark magic was allowed to flourish, the kingdom would never truly be safe.

And so, a practice began. The Shadowkind, now subjugated and enslaved, had their wings bound as soon as they fledged. Tight, constricting ropes that prevented their wings from ever reaching maturity, and therefore from ever unleashing the evil that lurked within.

This practice has continued for thousands of years, handed down from generation to generation of Sunborne rulers. It is a necessary cruelty, a harsh but vital measure to ensure the safety and prosperity of the kingdom.

For without the bindings, the Shadowkind would rise again. Their dark magic would return, and the realm would once more be plunged into an age of terror and despair.

This is the truth of our history, the dark secret that underlies the very foundation of our society. It is a heavy burden, a grim responsibility. But it is one the Sunborne, the descendants of that first great hero, must bear.

For the sake of the kingdom, for the sake of all fae, the Shadowkind must remain bound.

Their wings must never be allowed to spread.

And those with shadow magic must beware; for if the magic of shadows is used on a bound fae, their power will be unleashed.

Their demon form will rise.

This is the curse of the bindings.

Pre - Order

Pre-Order The Harlequin, the final book in The Fae Court Series HERE or alternatively head over to Amazon.

Join Alexis' Newsletter

Join Alexis Brooke's newsletter and stay up to date on all her upcoming books and get a NSFW digital image HERE or head over to www.alexisbrookbooks.com

Printed in Great Britain
by Amazon